FIVE GET
INTO
TROUBLE

Enid Blyton's

FIVE GET INTO TROUBLE

ILLUSTRATED BY JOLYNE KNOX

AWARD PUBLICATIONS

ISBN 0-86163-681-3

Text copyright © Darrell Waters Ltd 1949
Illustrations copyright © Hodder and Stoughton 1983

Enid Blyton's signature is a trademark of
Darrell Waters Limited

First published 1949 by Hodder and Stoughton Ltd
This edition 1983

This edition first published 1993 by Award Publications
Limited, Goodyear House, 52-56 Osnaburgh Street,
London NW1

Printed in Czech Republic

CONTENTS

1

Five make a holiday plan

'Really, Quentin, you are *most* difficult to cope with!' said Aunt Fanny to her husband.

The four children sat at the table, eating breakfast, and looking very interested. What had Uncle Quentin done now? Julian winked at Dick, and Anne kicked George under the table. Would Uncle Quentin explode into a temper, as he sometimes did?

Uncle Quentin held a letter in his hand, which his wife had just given back to him after she had read it. It was the letter that was causing all the trouble, Uncle Quentin frowned – and then decided not to explode. Instead he spoke quite mildly.

'Well, Fanny dear – how can I possibly be expected to remember exactly when the children's holidays come, and if they are going to be here with us or with your sister? You know I have my scientific work to do – and very important it is too, at the moment. *I* can't remember when the children's schools break up or go back!'

'You could always ask *me*,' said Aunt Fanny, exasper-

1

ated. 'Really, Quentin – have you forgotten how we discussed having Julian, Dick and Anne here these Easter holidays because they all enjoy Kirrin and the sea so much at this time of the year? You said you would arrange to go off to your conferences *after* they had had their holidays – not in the very middle of them!'

'But they've broken up so late!' said Uncle Quentin. 'I didn't know they were going to do that.'

'Well, but you know Easter came late this year, so they broke up late,' said Aunt Fanny, with a sigh.

'Father wouldn't think of that,' said George. 'What's the matter, Mother? Does Father want to go away in the middle of our holidays, or what?'

'Yes,' said Aunt Fanny, and she stretched out her hand for the letter again. 'Let me see – he would have to go off in two days' time – and I must certainly go with him. I can't possibly leave you children alone here, with nobody in the house. If Joanna were not ill it would be all right – but she won't be back for a week or two.'

Joanna was the cook. The children were all very fond of her, and had been sorry to find her missing when they had arrived for the holidays.

'We can look after ourselves,' said Dick. 'Anne is quite a good little cook.'

'I can help too,' said George. Her real name was Georgina, but everyone called her George. Her mother smiled.

'Oh George – last time you boiled an egg you left it in the saucepan till it boiled dry! I don't think the others would like your cooking very much.'

'It was just that I forgot the egg was there,' said George. 'I went to fetch the clock to time it, and on the way I remembered Timmy hadn't had his dinner, and . . .'

'Yes, we know all about that,' said her mother with a laugh. 'Timmy had his dinner, but your father had to go without his tea!'

3

'Woof,' said Timmy from under the table, hearing his name mentioned. He licked George's foot just to remind her he was there.

'Well, let's get back to the subject,' said Uncle Quentin, impatiently. 'I've got to go to these conferences, that's certain. I've to read some important papers there. You needn't come with me, Fanny – you can stay and look after the children.'

'Mother doesn't need to,' said George. 'We can do something we badly wanted to do, but thought we'd have to put off till the summer hols.'

'Oh *yes*,' said Anne, at once. 'So we could! Do let's!'

'Yes – I'd like that too,' said Dick.

'Well – *what* is it?' asked Aunt Fanny. 'I'm quite in the dark. If it's anything dangerous, I shall say no. So make up your minds about that!'

'When do we *ever* do anything dangerous?' cried George.

'Plenty of times,' said her mother. 'Now, what's this plan of yours?'

'It's nothing much,' said Julian. 'It's only that all our bikes happen to be in first-class order, Aunt Fanny, and you know you gave us two small tents for Christmas – so we just thought it would be great fun sometime to go off on our bikes, taking our tents with us – and do a little exploring round the countryside.'

'It's grand weather now – we could have fine fun,' said Dick. 'After all, you must have meant us to use the tents, Aunt Fanny! Here's our chance!'

'I meant you to use them in the garden, or on the beach,' said Aunt Fanny. 'Last time you went camping you had Mr Luffy with you to look after you. I don't think I like the idea of you going off by yourselves with tents.'

'Oh, Fanny, if *Julian* can't look after the others he must be a pretty feeble specimen,' said her husband, sounding impatient. 'Let them go! I'd bank on Julian any time to keep the others in order and see they were all safe and sound.'

'Thanks, Uncle,' said Julian, who was not used to compliments from his Uncle Quentin! He glanced round at the other children and grinned. 'Of course, it's easy to manage this little lot – though Anne sometimes is *very* difficult!'

Anne opened her mouth indignantly. She was the smallest and the only really manageable one. She caught Julian's grin – he was teasing her, of course. She grinned back. 'I promise to be easy to manage,' she said in an innocent voice to her Uncle Quentin.

He looked surprised. 'Well, I must say I should have thought that George was the only difficult one to . . .' he began, but stopped when he saw his wife's warning frown. George *was* difficult, but it didn't make her any less difficult if that fact was pointed out!

'Quentin, you never know when Julian is pulling your leg or not, do you?' said his wife. 'Well – if you *really* think Julian can be put in charge – and we can let them go off on a cycling tour – with their new tents . . .'

'Hurray! It's settled then!' yelled George, and began to thump Dick on the back in joy. 'We'll go off tomorrow. We'll . . .'

'GEORGE! There's no need to shout and thump like that,' said her mother. 'You know your father doesn't like it – and now you've excited Timmy too. Lie down, Timmy – there he's off round the room like a mad thing!'

Uncle Quentin got up to go. He didn't like it when meal-times turned into pandemonium. He almost fell over the excited Timmy, and disappeared thankfully out of the room. What a household it was when the four children and the dog were there!

'Oh Aunt Fanny – can we really go off tomorrow?' asked Anne, her eyes shining. 'It *is* such lovely April weather – honestly it's as hot as July. We hardly need to take any thick clothes with us.'

'Well, if you think that, you won't go,' said Aunt Fanny, firmly. 'It may be hot and sunny today – but you can never trust April to be the same two days together. It may be pouring tomorrow, and snowing on the next day! I shall have to give you money, Julian, so that you can go to an hotel any night the weather is bad.'

The four children immediately made up their minds that the weather would never be too bad!

'Won't it be fun?' said Dick. 'We can choose our own sleeping-place every night and put our tents there. We can bike half the night if it's moonlight, and we want to!'

'Ooooh – biking in moonlight – I've never done that,' said Anne. 'It sounds super.'

'Well – it's a good thing there is something you want to do while we are away,' said Aunt Fanny. 'Dear me – I've been married all these years to Quentin – and still he makes this kind of muddle without my knowing! Well, well – we'd better get busy today, and decide what you're to take.'

Everything suddenly seemed very exciting. The four children rushed to do their morning jobs of making the beds and tidying their rooms, talking at the tops of their voices.

'Who would have thought we'd be off on our own tomorrow!' said Dick, pulling his sheets and blankets up in a heap together.

'Dick! *I'll* make your bed,' cried Anne, shocked to see it made in such a hurried way. 'You can't possibly make it like that!'

Oh, *can't* I!' cried Dick. 'You just wait and see! And what's more I'm making Julian's like that too, so you clear off and do your own, Anne – tuck in every corner, smooth the pillow, pat the eiderdown – do what you like with your own bed, but leave me to make mine my own way! Wait till we're off on our biking tour – you won't want to bother about beds then – you'll roll up your sleeping-bag and that will be that!'

He finished his bed as he spoke, dragging on the cover all crooked, and stuffing his pyjamas under the pillow. Anne laughed and went to make her own. She was excited too. The days stretched before her, sunny, full of strange places, unknown woods, big and little hills, chattering streams, wayside picnics, biking in the moonlight – did Dick really mean that? How wizard!

They were all very busy that day, packing up into rucksacks the things they would need, folding up the tents into as small a compass as possible to tie on to their carriers, ferreting in the larder for food to take, looking out the maps they would want.

Timmy knew they were going off somewhere, and, of course, felt certain he was going too, so he was as excited as they were, barking and thumping his tail, and generally getting into everyone's way all day long. But nobody minded. Timmy was one of them, one of the 'Five', he could do almost everything but speak – it was quite unthinkable to go anywhere without dear old Timmy.

'I suppose Timothy can keep up with you all right, when you bike for miles?' Aunt Fanny asked Julian.

'Goodness yes,' said Julian. 'He never minds how far we go. I hope you won't worry about us, Aunt Fanny. You know what a good guard Timmy is.'

'Yes – I know,' said his aunt. 'I wouldn't be letting you go off like this with such an easy mind if I didn't know Timmy would be with you! He's as good as any grown-up at looking after you!'

'Woof, woof,' agreed Timmy. George laughed. 'He says he's as good as *two* grown-ups, Mother!' she said, and Timmy thumped his big tail on the floor.

'Woof, woof, *woof*,' he said. Which meant, 'Not two – but *three*!'

2

Away on their own

They were all ready the next day. Everything was neatly packed and strapped to the bicycles, except for the rucksacks, which each child was to carry on his or her back. The baskets held a variety of food for that day, but when it had been eaten Julian was to buy what they needed.

'I suppose all their brakes are in order?' said Uncle Quentin, thinking he ought to take some interest in the proceedings, and remembering that when *he* was a boy and had a bicycle, the brakes would never work.

'Oh Uncle Quentin – of course they're all right,' said Dick. 'We'd never dream of going out on our bikes if the brakes and things weren't in order. The Highway Code is very strict about things like that, you know – and so are we!'

Uncle Quentin looked as if he had never even heard of the Highway Code. It was quite likely he hadn't. He lived in a world of his own, a world of theories and figures and diagrams – and he was eager to get back to it! However, he waited politely for the children to make last-minute adjustments, and then they were ready.

'Good-bye, Aunt Fanny! I'm afraid we shan't be able to write to you, as you won't be able to get in touch with us to let us know where you get fixed up. Never mind, enjoy yourselves,' said Julian.

'Good-bye, Mother! Don't worry about us – we'll be having a jolly good time!' called George.

'Good-bye, Aunt Fanny; good-bye, Uncle Quentin!'

'So long, Uncle! Aunt Fanny, we're off!'

And so they were, cycling down the lane that led away from Kirrin Cottage. Their aunt and uncle stood at the gate, waving till the little party had disappeared round the corner in the sunshine. Timmy was loping along beside George's bicycle, on his long, strong legs, overjoyed at the idea of a really good run.

'Well, we're off,' said Julian, as they rounded the corner. 'What a bit of luck, going off like this by ourselves. Good old Uncle Quentin! I'm glad he made that muddle.'

'Don't let's ride too many miles the first day – I always get so stiff if we do.'

'We're not going to,' said Dick. 'Whenever you feel tired just say so – it doesn't matter where we stop!'

The morning was very warm. Soon the children began to feel wet with perspiration. They had sweaters on and they took them off, stuffing them in their baskets. George looked more like a boy than ever, with her short curly hair blown up by the wind. All of them wore shorts and thin jerseys except Julian, who had on jeans. He rolled up the sleeves of his jersey, and the others did the same.

They covered mile after mile, enjoying the sun and the wind. Timmy galloped beside them, untiring, his long pink tongue hanging out. He ran on the grassy edge of the road when there was one. He really was a very sensible dog!

They stopped at a tiny village called Manlington-

Tovey. It had only one general store, but it sold practically everything – or seemed to! 'Hope it sells ginger-beer!' said Julian. 'My tongue's hanging out like Timmy's!'

The little shop sold lemonade, orangeade, lime juice, grape-fruit juice and ginger-beer. It was really difficult to choose which to have. It also sold ice-creams, and soon the children were sitting drinking ginger-beer and lime-juice mixed, and eating delicious ices.

'Timmy must have an ice,' said George. 'He does so love them. Don't you, Timmy?'

'Woof,' said Timmy, and gulped his ice down in two big, gurgly licks.

'It's really a waste of ice-creams to give them to Timmy,' said Anne. 'He hardly has time to taste them, he gobbles them so. No, Timmy, get down. I'm going to finish up every single bit of mine, and there won't be even a lick for you!'

Timmy went off to drink from a bowl of water that the shopwoman had put down for him. He drank and he drank, then he flopped down, panting.

The children took a bottle of ginger-beer each with them when they went off again. They meant to have it with their lunch. Already they were beginning to think with pleasure of eating the sandwiches put up into neat packets for them.

Anne saw some cows pulling at the grass in a meadow as they passed. 'It must be awful to be a cow and eat nothing but tasteless grass,' she called to George. 'Think what a cow misses – never tastes an egg and lettuce sandwich, never eats a chocolate eclair, never has a boiled egg – and can't even drink a glass of ginger-beer! Poor cows!'

George laughed. 'You do think of silly things, Anne,' she said. 'Now you've made me want my lunch all the more – talking about egg sandwiches and ginger-beer! I know Mother made us egg sandwiches – and sardine ones too.'

10

'It's no good,' chimed in Dick, leading the way into a little copse, his bicycle wobbling dangerously, 'it's no good – we can't go another inch if you girls are going to jabber about food all the time. Julian, what about lunch?'

It was a lovely picnic, that first one in the copse. There were clumps of primroses all round, and from somewhere nearby came the sweet scent of hidden violets. A thrush was singing madly on a hazel tree, with two chaffinches calling 'pink-pink' every time he stopped.

'Band and decorations laid on,' said Julian, waving his hand towards the singing birds and the primroses. 'Very nice too. We just want a waiter to come and present us with a menu!'

A rabbit lolloped near, its big ears standing straight up inquiringly. 'Ah – the waiter!' said Julian, at once. 'What have you to offer us today, Bunny? A nice rabbit-pie?'

The rabbit scampered off at top speed. It had caught the smell of Timmy nearby and was panic-stricken. The children laughed, because it seemed as if it was the mention of rabbit-pie that had sent it away. Timmy stared at the disappearing rabbit, but made no move to go after it.

'Well, *Timmy*! That's the first time you've ever let a rabbit go off on its own,' said Dick. 'You *must* be hot and tired. Got anything for him to eat, George?'

'Of course,' said George. 'I made his sandwiches myself.'

And so she had! She had bought sausage meat at the butchers and had actually made Timmy twelve sandwiches with it, all neatly cut and packed.

The others laughed. George never minded taking trouble over Timmy. He wolfed his sandwiches eagerly, and thumped his tail hard on the mossy ground. They all sat and munched happily, perfectly contented to be together out in the open air, eating a wonderful lunch.

Anne gave a scream. 'George! Look what you're doing! You're eating one of Timmy's sandwiches!'

'Urhh!' said George. 'I thought it tasted a bit strong. I must have given Timmy one of mine and taken his instead. Sorry, Tim!'

'Woof,' said Tim politely, and accepted another of his sandwiches.

'At the rate he eats them he wouldn't really notice if he had twenty or fifty,' remarked Julian. 'He's had all his now, hasn't he? Well, look out, everybody – he'll be after ours. Aha – the band has struck up again!'

Everyone listened to the thrush. 'Mind how you go,' sang the thrush. 'Mind how you go! Mind how you do-it, do-it, do-it!'

'Sounds like a Safety First poster,' said Dick, and settled down with his head on a cushion of moss. 'All right, old bird – we'll mind how we go – but we're going to have a bit of a snooze now, so don't play the band too loudly!'

'It *would* be a good idea to have a bit of a rest,' said Julian, yawning. 'We've done pretty well, so far. We don't want to tire ourselves out the very first day. Get off my legs, Timmy – you're frightfully heavy with all those sandwiches inside you.'

Timmy removed himself. He went to George and flumped himself down beside her, licking her face. She pushed him away.

'Don't be so licky,' she said, sleepily, 'just be on guard like a good dog, and see that nobody comes along and steals our bikes.'

Timmy knew what 'on guard' meant, of course. He sat up straight when he heard the words, and looked carefully all round, sniffing as he did so. Anyone about? No. Not a sight, sound or smell of any stranger. Timmy lay down again, one ear cocked, and one eye very slightly open. George always thought it was marvellous the way he could be asleep with one ear and eye and awake with the others. She was about to say this to Dick and Julian when she saw that they were sound asleep.

She fell asleep too. Nobody came to disturb them. A small robin hopped near inquisitively, and, with his head on one side, considered whether or not it would be a good thing to pull a few hairs out of Timmy's tail to line his new nest. The slit in Timmy's awake-eye widened a little

13

– woe betide the robin if he tried any funny tricks on Timmy!

The robin flew off. The thrush sang a little more, and the rabbit came out again. Timmy's eye opened wide. The rabbit fled. Timmy gave a tiny snore. Was he awake or was he asleep? The rabbit wasn't going to wait and find out!

It was half past three when they all awoke one by one. Julian looked at his watch. 'It's almost tea-time!' he said, and Anne gave a little squeal.

'Oh no – why we've only just had lunch, and I'm still as full as can be!'

Julian grinned. 'It's all right. We'll go by our tummies for our meals, not by our watches, Anne. Come on, get up! We'll go without you if you don't.'

They wheeled their bicycles out of the primrose copse and mounted again. The breeze was lovely to feel on their faces. Anne gave a little groan.

'Oh dear – I feel a bit stiff already. Do you mean to go very many miles more, Ju?'

'No, not many,' said Julian. 'I thought we'd have tea somewhere when we feel like it – and then do a bit of shopping for our supper and breakfast – and then hunt about for a really good place to put up our tents for the night. I found a little lake on the map, and I thought we could have a swim in it if we can find it.'

This all sounded very good indeed. George felt she could cycle for miles if a swim in a lake was at the end of it.

'That's a very nice plan of yours,' she said, approvingly. 'Very nice indeed. I think our whole tour ought to be planned round lakes – so that we can always have a swim, night and morning!'

'Woof,' said Timmy, running beside George's bicycle. 'Woof!'

'Timmy agrees too,' said George, with a laugh. 'But oh dear – I don't believe he brought his bathing-towel!'

3

A lovely day – and a lovely night

The five of them had a lovely time that evening. They had tea about half past five, and then bought what they wanted for supper and breakfast. New rolls, anchovy paste, a big round jam-tart in a cardboard box, oranges, lime-juice, a fat lettuce and some ham sandwiches – it seemed a very nice assortment indeed.

'Let's hope we don't eat it all for supper, and have no breakfast left,' said George, packing the sandwiches into her basket. 'Get down, Timmy. These sandwiches are not for you. I've bought you a whacking big bone – *that* will keep you busy for hours!'

'Well, don't let him have it when we settle down for the night,' said Anne. 'He makes such a row, crunching and munching. He'd keep me awake.'

'*Nothing* would keep *me* awake tonight,' said Dick. 'I believe I could sleep through an earthquake. I'm already thinking kindly of my sleeping-bag.'

'I don't think we need to put up our tents tonight,' said Julian, looking up at the perfectly clear sky. 'I'll ask someone what the weather forecast was on the radio at six.

Honestly I think we could just snuggle into our sleeping-bags and have the sky for a roof.'

'How smashing!' said Anne. 'I'd love to lie and look at the stars.'

The weather forecast was good. 'Fine and clear and mild'.

'Good,' said Julian. 'That will save us a lot of trouble – we don't even need to unpack our tents. Come on – have we got everything now? Does anyone feel as if we ought to buy any more food?'

The baskets were all full. Nobody thought it advisable to try and get anything more into them.

'We could get lots more in if Timmy would only carry his own bones,' said Anne. 'Half my basket is crammed with enormous bones for him. Why can't you rig up something so that Timmy could carry his own food, George? I'm sure he's clever enough.'

'Yes, he's clever enough,' said George. 'But he's much too greedy, Anne. You know that. He'd stop and eat all his food at once if he had to carry it. Dogs seem to be able to eat anything at any time.'

'They're lucky,' said Dick. 'Wish I could. But I just *have* to pause between my meals!'

'Now for the lake,' said Julian, folding up the map which he had just been examining. 'It's only about five miles away. It's called the Green Pool, but it looks a good bit bigger than a pool. I could do with a bathe. I'm so hot and sticky.'

They came to the lake at about half past seven. It was in a lovely place, and had beside it a small hut which was obviously used in summer-time for bathers to change into bathing-suits. Now it was locked, and curtains were drawn across the windows.

'I suppose we can go in for a dip if we like?' said Dick rather doubtfully. 'We shan't be trespassing or anything, shall we?'

'No. It doesn't say anything about being private,' said Julian. 'The water won't be very warm, you know, because it's only mid-April! But after all, we're used to cold baths every morning, and I daresay the sun has taken the chill off the lake. Come on – let's get into bathing-things.'

They changed behind the bushes and then ran down to the lake. The water was certainly very cold indeed. Anne skipped in and out, and wouldn't do any more than that.

George joined the boys in a swim, and they all came out glowing and laughing. 'Brrr, that was cold!' said Dick. 'Come on – let's have a sharp run. Look at Anne – dressed already. Timmy, where are you? *You* don't mind the cold water, do you?'

They all tore up and down the little paths by the Green Pool like mad things. Anne was getting the supper ready. The sun had disappeared now, and although the evening was still very mild the radiant warmth of the day had gone. Anne was glad of her sweater.

'Good old Anne,' said Dick, when at last he and the others joined her, dressed again, with their sweaters on for warmth. 'Look, she's got the food all ready. Proper little housewife, aren't you, Anne? I bet if we stayed here for more than one night Anne would have made some kind of larder, and have arranged a good place to wash everything – and be looking for somewhere to keep her dusters and broom!'

'You're so *silly*, Dick,' said Anne. 'You ought to be glad I like messing about with the food and getting it ready for you. Oh TIMMY! Shoo! Get away! Look at him, he's shaken millions and millions of drops of lakewater all over the food. You ought to have dried him, George. You know how he shakes himself after a swim.'

'Sorry,' said George. 'Tim, say you're sorry. Why must you be so *violent* about everything? If I shook myself like that my ears and fingers would fly off into the air!'

It was a lovely meal, sitting there in the evening light,

watching the first stars come out in the sky. The children and Timmy were all tired but happy. This was the beginning of their trip – and beginnings were always lovely – the days stretched out before you endlessly, and somehow you felt certain that the sun would shine every single day!

They were not long in snuggling into their sleeping-bags when they had finished the meal. They had set them all together in a row, so that they could talk if they wanted to. Timmy was thrilled. He walked solemnly across the whole lot, and was greeted with squeals and threats.

'Timmy! How dare you! When I've had such a big supper too!'

'TIMMY! You brute! You put all your great big feet down on me at once!'

'George, you *really* might stop Timmy from walking all over us like that! I only hope he's not going to do it all night long.'

Timmy looked surprised at the shouts. He settled down beside George, after a vain attempt to get into her sleeping-bag with her. George turned her face away from his licks.

'Oh Timmy, I do love you but I wish you wouldn't make my face so wet. Julian, look at that glorious star – like a little round lamp. What is it?'

'It's not a star really – it's Venus, one of the planets,' said Julian, sleepily. 'But it's called the Evening Star. Fancy you not knowing that, George. Don't they teach you anything at your school?'

George tried to kick Julian through her sleeping-bag, but she couldn't. She gave it up and yawned so loudly that she set all the others yawning too.

Anne fell asleep first. She was the smallest and was more easily tired with long walks and rides than the others, though she always kept up with them valiantly. George gazed unblinkingly at the bright evening star for a

minute and then fell asleep suddenly. Julian and Dick talked quietly for a few minutes. Timmy was quite silent. He was tired out with his miles and miles of running.

Nobody stirred at all that night, not even Timmy. He took no notice of a horde of rabbits who played not far off. He hardly pricked an ear when an owl hooted nearby. He didn't even stir when a beetle ran over his head.

But if George had waked and spoken his name Timmy

would have been wide awake at once, standing over George and licking her, whining gently! George was the centre of his world, night and day.

The next day was fair and bright. It was lovely to wake up and feel the warm sun on their cheeks, and hear a thrush singing his heart out. 'It might be the very same thrush,' thought Dick, drowsily. 'He's saying, "Mind how you do-it, do-it, do-it!" just like the other one did.'

Anne sat up cautiously. She wondered if she should get up and have breakfast ready for the others – or would they want a bathe first?

Julian sat up next and yawned as he wriggled himself half out of his sleeping-bag. He grinned at Anne.

'Hallo,' he said. 'Had a good night? I feel fine this morning!'

'I feel rather stiff,' said Anne. 'But it will soon wear off. Hallo, George – you awake?'

George grunted and snuggled down farther in her sleeping-bag. Timmy pawed at her, whining. He wanted her to get up and go for a run with him.

'Shut up, Timmy,' said George from the depth of her bag. 'I'm asleep!'

'I'm going for a bathe,' said Julian. 'Anyone else coming?'

'I won't,' said Anne. 'It will be too cold for me this morning. George doesn't seem to want to, either. You two boys go by yourselves. I'll have breakfast ready for you when you come back. Sorry I shan't be able to have anything hot for you to drink – but we didn't bring a kettle or anything like that.'

Julian and Dick went off to the Green Pool, still looking sleepy. Anne got out of her sleeping-bag and dressed quickly. She decided to go down to the pool with her sponge and flannel and wake herself up properly with the cold water. George was still in her sleeping-bag.

The two boys were almost at the pool. Ah, now they

could see it between the trees, shining a bright emerald green. It looked very inviting indeed.

They suddenly saw a bicycle standing beside a tree. They looked at it in astonishment. It wasn't one of theirs. It must belong to someone else.

Then they heard splashings from the pool, and they hurried down to it. Was someone else bathing?

A boy was in the pool, his golden head shining wet and smooth in the morning sun. He was swimming powerfully across the pool, leaving long ripples behind him as he went. He suddenly saw Dick and Julian, and swam over to them.

'Hallo,' he said, wading out of the water. 'You come for a swim too? Nice pool of mine, isn't it?'

'What do you mean? It isn't really your pool, is it? said Julian.

'Well – it belongs to my father, Thurlow Kent,' said the boy.

Both Julian and Dick had heard of Thurlow Kent, one of the richest men in the country. Julian looked doubtfully at the boy.

'If it's a private pool we won't use it,' he said.

'Oh come on!' cried the boy, and splashed cold water all over them. 'Race you to the other side!'

And off all three of them went, cleaving the green waters with their strong brown arms – what a fine beginning to a sunny day!

4

Richard

Anne was astonished to find three boys in the Green Pool instead of two. She stood by the water with her sponge and flannel, staring. Who was the third boy?

The three came back to the side of the pool where Anne stood. She looked at the strange boy shyly. He was not much older than she was, and not as big as Julian or Dick, but he was sturdily made, and had laughing blue eyes she liked. He smoothed back his dripping hair.

'This your sister?' he said to Julian and Dick. 'Hallo there!'

'Hallo,' said Anne and smiled. 'What's your name?'

'Richard,' he said. 'Richard Kent. What's yours?'

'Anne,' said Anne. 'We're on a biking tour.'

The boys had had no time to introduce themselves. They were still panting from their swim.

'I'm Julian and he's Dick, my brother,' said Julian, out of breath. 'I say – I hope we're not trespassing on your land as well as on your water!'

Richard grinned. 'Well, you are as a matter of fact. But

I give you free permission! You can borrow my pool and my land as much as you like!'

'Oh thanks,' said Anne. 'I suppose it's your father's property? It didn't say "Private" or anything, so we didn't know. Would you like to come and have breakfast with us? If you'll dress with the others they'll bring you to where we camped last night.'

She sponged her face and washed her hands in the pool, hearing the boys chattering behind the bushes where they had left their clothes. Then she sped back to their sleeping-place, meaning to tidy up the bags they had slept in, and put out breakfast neatly. But George was still fast asleep in her bag, her head showing at the top with its mass of short curls that made her look like a boy.

'George! Do wake up. Somebody's coming to breakfast,' said Anne, shaking her.

George shrugged away crossly, not believing her. It was just a trick to make her get up and help with the breakfast! Anne left her. All right – let her be found in her sleeping-bag if she liked!

She began to unpack the food and set it out neatly. What a good thing they had brought two extra bottles of lime-juice. Now they could offer Richard one.

The three boys came up, their wet hair plastered down. Richard spotted George in the bag as Timmy came over to meet him. He fondled Timmy who, smelling that other dogs had been round Richard at home, sniffed him over with great interest.

'Who's that still asleep?' asked Richard.

'That's George,' said Anne. 'Too sleepy to wake up! Come on – I've got breakfast ready. Would you like to start off with rolls and anchovy and lettuce? And there's lime-juice if you want it.'

George heard Richard's voice, as he sat talking with the others and was astonished. Who was that? She sat up, blinking, her hair tousled and short. Richard honestly thought she was a boy. She looked like one and she was called George!

'Top of the morning to you, George,' he said. 'Hope I'm not eating your share of the breakfast.'

'Who are you?' demanded George. The boys told her.

'I live about three miles away,' said the boy. 'I biked over here this morning for a swim. I say – that reminds me – I'd better bring my bike up here and put it where I can see it. I've had two stolen already through not having them under my eye.'

He shot off to get his bike. George took the opportunity of getting out of her sleeping-bag and rushed off to dress. She was back before Richard was, eating her breakfast. He wheeled his bicycle as he came.

'Got it all right,' he said, and flung it down beside him. 'Don't want to have to tell my father this one's gone, like the others. He's pretty fierce.'

'My father's a bit fierce too,' said George.

'Does he whip you?' asked Richard, giving Timmy a nice little titbit of roll and anchovy paste.

'Of course not,' said George. 'He's just got a temper, that's all.'

'Mine's got tempers and rages and furies, and if anyone offends him or does him a wrong he's like an elephant – never forgets,' said Richard. 'He's made plenty of enemies in his lifetime. Sometimes he's had his life threatened, and he's had to take a bodyguard about with him.'

This all sounded extremely thrilling. Dick half-wished he had a father like that. I would be nice to talk to the other boys at school about his father's 'bodyguard'.

'What's his bodyguard like?' asked Anne, full of curiosity.

'Oh, they vary. But they're all big hefty fellows – they look like ruffians, and probably are,' said Richard, enjoying the interest the others were taking in him. 'One he had last year was awful – he had the thickest lips you ever saw, and such a big nose that when you saw him sideways you really thought he'd put a false one on just for fun.'

'Gracious!' said Anne. 'He sounds horrible. Has your father still got him?'

'No. He did something that annoyed Dad – I don't know what – and after a perfectly furious row my father chucked him out,' said Richard. 'That was the end of *him* . Jolly good thing too. I hated him. He used to kick the dogs around terribly.'

'*Oh!* What a beast!' said George, horrified. She put her arm round Timmy as if she was afraid somebody might suddenly kick him around too.

Julian and Dick wondered whether to believe all this. They came to the conclusion that the tales Richard told were very much exaggerated, and they listened with amusement, but not with such horror as the two girls, who hung on every word that Richard said.

'Where's your father now?' said Anne. 'Has he got a special bodyguard this very moment?'

'Rather! He's in America this week, but he's flying home soon – plus bodyguard,' said Richard, drinking the last of his lime-juice from the bottle. 'U..mm, that's good. I say, aren't you lucky to be allowed to go off alone like this on your bikes – and sleep where you like. My mother never will let *me* – she's always afraid something will happen to me.'

'Perhaps you'd better have a bodyguard too,' suggested Julian, slyly.

'I'd soon give him the slip,' said Richard. 'As a matter of fact I *have* got a kind of a bodyguard.'

'Who? Where?' asked Anne, looking all round as if she expected some enormous ruffian suddenly to appear.

'Well – he's supposed to be my holiday tutor,' said Richard, tickling Timmy round the ears. 'He's called Lomax and he's pretty awful. I'm supposed to tell him every time I go out – just as if I was a kid like Anne here.'

Anne was indignant. 'I don't have to tell anybody when I want to go off on my own,' she said.

'Actually I don't think we'd be allowed to rush off completely on our own unless we had old Timmy,' said Dick, honestly. 'He's better than any ruffianly bodyguard or holiday tutor. I wonder *you* don't have a dog.'

'Oh, I've got about five,' said Richard, airily.

'What are their names?' asked George, disbelievingly.

'Er – Bunter, Biscuit, Brownie, Bones – and er – Bonzo,' said Richard, with a grin.

'Silly names,' said George, scornfully. 'Fancy calling a dog *Biscuit*. You must be cracked.'

'You shut up,' said Richard, with a sudden scowl. 'I don't stand people telling me I'm cracked.'

'Well, you'll have to stand *me* telling you,' said George. 'I *do* think it's cracked to call a dog, a nice, decent dog, by a name like *Biscuit*!'

'I'll fight you then,' said Richard, surprisingly, and stood up. 'Come on – you stand up.'

George leapt to her feet. Julian shot out a hand and pulled her down again.

'None of that,' he said to Richard. 'You ought to be ashamed of yourself.'

'Why?' flared out Richard, whose face had gone very red. Evidently he and his father shared the same fierceness of temper!

'Well, you don't fight *girls*,' said Julian, scornfully. 'Or do you? Correct me if I'm wrong.'

Richard stared at him in amazement. 'What do you mean?' he said. 'Girls? Of course I don't fight girls. No decent boy hits a girl – but it's this boy here I want to fight – what do you call him? – George.'

To his great surprise Julian, Dick and Anne roared with laughter. Timmy barked madly too, pleased at the sudden

ending of the quarrel. Only George looked mutinous and cross.

'What's up now?' asked Richard, aggressively. 'What's all the fun and games about?'

'Richard, George isn't a boy – she's a *girl*,' explained Dick at last. 'My goodness – she was just about to accept your challenge and fight you, too – two fierce little fox-terriers having a scrap!'

Richard's mouth fell open in an even greater astonishment. He blushed redder than ever. He looked sheepishly at George.

'Are you *really* a girl?' he said. 'You behave so like a boy – and you look like one too. Sorry, George. Is your name *really* George?'

'No – Georgina,' said George, thawing a little at Richard's awkward apology, and pleased that he had honestly thought her a boy. She did so badly want to be a boy and not a girl.

'Good thing I *didn't* fight you,' said Richard, fervently. 'I should have knocked you flat!'

'Well, I like *that*!' said George, flaring up all over again. Julian pushed her back with his hand.

'Now shut up, you two, and don't behave like idiots. Where's the map? It's time we had a squint at it and decided what we are going to do for today – how far we're going to ride, and where we're making for by the evening.'

Fortunately George and Richard both gave in with a good grace. Soon all six heads – Timmy's too – were bent over the map. Julian made his decision.

'We'll make for Middlecombe Woods – see, there they are on the map. That's decided then – it'll be a jolly nice ride.'

It might be a nice ride – but it was going to be something very much more than that!

5

Six instead of five

'Look here,' said Richard, when they had tidied up everything, buried their bits of litter, and looked to see that no one had got a puncture in a tyre. 'Look here – I've got an aunt who lives in the direction of those woods – if I can get my mother to say I can come with you, will you let me? I can go and see my aunt on the way, then.'

Julian looked at Richard doubtfully. He wasn't very sure if Richard really *would* go and ask permission.

'Well – if you aren't too long about it,' he said. 'Of course we don't mind you coming with us. We can drop you at your aunt's on the way.'

'I'll go straight off now and ask my mother,' said Richard, eagerly, and he ran for his bicycle. 'I'll meet you at Croker's Corner – you saw it on the map. That will save time, because then I shan't have to come back here – it's not much farther than my home.'

'Right,' said Julian. 'I've got to adjust my brakes, and that will take ten minutes or so. You'll have time to go home and ask permission, and join us later. We'll wait for you; at least we'll wait for ten minutes, at Croker's Corner. If you don't turn up we'll know you didn't get permission. Tell your mother we'll leave you safely at your aunt's.'

Richard shot off on his bicycle, looking excited. Anne began to clear up, and George helped her. Timmy got in everyone's way, sniffing about for dropped crumbs.

'Anyone would think he was half-starved!' said Anne. 'He had a lot more breakfast than I had. Timmy, if you walk through my legs again I'll tie you up!'

Julian adjusted his brakes with Dick's help. In about fifteen minutes they were ready to set off. They had planned where to stop to buy food for their lunch, and although the journey to Middlecombe Woods was a longer trip than they had made the day before, they felt able to cope with more miles on the second day. Timmy was eager to set off too. He was a big dog, and enjoyed all the exercise he was getting.

'It'll take a bit of your fat off,' said Dick to Timmy. 'We don't like fat dogs, you know. They waddle and they puff.'

'Dick! Timmy's *never* been fat!' said George, indignantly, and then stopped as she saw Dick's grin. He was pulling her leg as usual. She kicked herself. Why did she always rise like that, when Dick teased her through Timmy? She gave him a friendly punch.

They all mounted their bicycles. Timmy ran ahead, pleased. They came to a lane and rode down it, avoiding the ruts. They came out into a road. It was not a main road, for the children didn't like those; they were too full of traffic and dust. They liked the shady lanes or the country roads where they met only a few carts or a farmer's car.

'Now, don't let's miss Croker's Corner,' said Julian. 'It should be along this way somewhere, according to the map. George, if you get into ruts like that you'll be thrown off.'

'All right, I know that!' said George. 'I only got into one because Timmy swerved across my wheel. He's after a rabbit or something. Timmy! Don't get left behind, you idiot.'

Timmy bounded reluctantly after the little party. Exercise was wonderful, but it did mean leaving a lot of marvellous wayside smells unsniffed at. It was a dreadful waste of smells, Timmy thought.

They came to Croker's Corner sooner than they thought. The signpost proclaimed the name – and there, leaning against the post, sitting on his bicycle was Richard, beaming at them.

'You've been jolly quick, getting back home and then on to here,' said Julian. 'What did your mother say?'

'She didn't mind a bit so long as I was with *you*,' said Richard. 'I can go to my aunt's for the night, she said.'

'Haven't you brought pyjamas or anything with you?' asked Dick.

'There are always spare ones at my aunt's,' explained Richard. 'Hurray – it will be marvellous to be out on my own all day with you – no Mr Lomax to bother me with this and that. Come on!'

They all cycled on together. Richard would keep trying to ride three abreast, and Julian had to warn him that cyclists were not allowed to do that. 'I don't care!' sang Richard, who seemed in very high spirits. 'Who is there to stop us, anyway?'

'*I* shall stop you,' said Julian, and Richard ceased grinning at once. Julian could sound very stern when he liked. Dick winked at George, and she winked back. They had both come to the conclusion that Richard was very spoilt and liked his own way. Well, he wouldn't get it if he came up against old Julian!

They stopped at eleven for ice-creams and drinks. Richard seemed to have a lot of money. He insisted on buying ice-creams for all of them, even Timmy.

Once again they bought food for their lunch – new bread, farm-house butter, cream cheese, crisp lettuce, fat red radishes and a bunch of spring onions. Richard bought a magnificent chocolate cake he saw in a first-class cake-shop.

'Gracious! That must have cost you a fortune!' said Anne. 'How are we going to carry it?'

'Woof,' said Timmy longingly.

'No, I certainly shan't let *you* carry it,' said Anne. 'Oh dear – we'll have to cut it in half, I think, and two people can share the carrying. It's such an enormous cake.'

On they went again, getting into the real country now, with villages few and far between. A farm here and there showed up on the hillsides, with cows and sheep and fowls. It was a peaceful, quiet scene, with the sun spilling down over everything, and the blue April sky above, patched with great white cotton-wool clouds.

'This is grand,' said Richard. 'I say, doesn't Timmy *ever* get tired? He's panting like anything now.'

'Yes. I think we ought to find somewhere for our lunch,' said Julian, looking at his watch. 'We've done a very good run this morning. Of course a lot of the way has been downhill. This afternoon we'll probably be slower, because we'll be getting into hilly country.'

They found a spot to picnic in. They chose the sunny side of a hedge, looking downhill into a small valley. Sheep and lambs were in the field they sat in. The lambs were very inquisitive, and one came right up to Anne and bleated.

'Do you want a bit of my bread?' asked Anne, and held it out to the lamb. Timmy watched indignantly. Fancy handing out food to those silly little creatures! He growled a little, and George shushed him.

Soon all the lambs were crowding round, quite unafraid, and one even tried to put its little front legs up on to George's shoulders! That was too much for Timmy! He gave such a sudden, fierce growl that all the lambs shot off at once.

'Oh, don't be so jealous, Timmy,' said George. 'Take this sandwich and behave yourself. Now you've frightened away the lambs, and they won't come back.'

They all ate the food and then drank their lime-juice and ginger-beer. The sun was very hot. Soon they would all be burnt brown – and it was only April. How marvellous! Julian thought lazily that they were really lucky to have such weather – it would be awful to have to bike along all day in the pouring rain.

Once again the children snoozed in the afternoon sun, Richard too – and the little lambs skipped nearer and nearer. One actually leapt on to Julian as he slept, and he sat upright with a jerk. 'Timmy!' he began, 'if you leap on me again like that I'll . . .'

But it wasn't Timmy, it was a lamb! Julian laughed to himself. He sat for a few minutes and watched the little white creatures playing 'I'm king of the castle' with an old coop, then he lay down again.

'Are we anywhere near your aunt's house?' Julian asked Richard, when they once more mounted their bicycles.

'If we're anywhere near Great Giddings, we shall soon be there,' said Richard, riding without his handlebars and almost ending up in the ditch. 'I didn't notice it on the map.'

Julian tried to remember. 'Yes – we should be at Great Giddings round about tea-time – say five o'clock or thereabouts. We'll leave you at your aunt's house for tea if you like.'

'Oh no, thank you,' said Richard, quickly. 'I'd much rather have tea with *you*. I *do* wish I could come on this tour with you. I suppose I couldn't possibly? You could telephone my mother.'

'Don't be an ass,' said Julian. 'You can have tea with us if you like – but we drop you at your aunt's as arranged, see? No nonsense about that.'

They came to Great Giddings at about ten past five.

Although it was called Great it was really very small. There was a little tea-place that said 'Home-made cakes and jams', so they went there for tea.

The woman who kept it was a plump, cheerful soul, fond of children. She guessed she would make very little out of the tea she served to five healthy children – but that didn't matter! She set to work to cut three big plates of well-buttered slices of bread, put out apricot jam, raspberry, and strawberry, and a selection of home-made buns that made the children's mouths water.

She knew Richard quite well, because he had sometimes been to her cottage with his aunt.

'I suppose you'll be going to stay with her tonight?' she said to Richard, and he nodded, his mouth full of ginger cake. It was a lovely tea. Anne felt as if she wouldn't be able to eat any supper at all that night! Even Timmy seemed to have satisfied his enormous appetite.

'I think we ought to pay you double price for our gorgeous tea,' said Julian, but the woman wouldn't hear of it. No, no – it was lovely to see them all enjoying her cakes; she didn't want double price!

'Some people are so *awfully* nice and generous,' said Anne, as they mounted their bicycles to ride off again. 'You just can't help liking them. I do hope I can cook like that when I grow up.'

'If you do, Julian and I will always live with you and not dream of getting married!' said Dick, promptly, and they all laughed.

'Now for Richard's aunt,' said Julian. 'Do you know where the house is, Richard?'

'Yes – that's it over there,' said Richard, and rode up to a gate. 'Well, thanks awfully for your company. I hope I'll see you again soon! I have a feeling I shall! Good-bye!'

He rode up the drive and disappeared. 'What a sudden good-bye!' said George, puzzled. 'Isn't he *odd*?'

6

Odd happenings

They all thought it really was a little odd to disappear so suddenly like that, with just a casual good-bye. Julian wondered if he ought to have gone with him and delivered him safely on the door-step.

'Don't be an ass, Julian,' said Dick, scornfully. 'What *do* you think can happen to him from the front gate to the front door!'

'Nothing, of course. It's just that I don't trust that young fellow,' said Julian. 'You know I really wasn't sure he had asked his mother if he could come with us, to tell you the truth.'

'I thought that too,' said Anne. 'He did get to Croker's Corner so very quickly, didn't he? – and he had quite a long way to go really, and he had to find his mother, and talk to her, and all that.'

'Yes. I've half a mind to pop up to the aunt's house and see if she expected him,' said Julian. But on second thoughts he didn't go. He would feel so silly if the aunt was there with Richard, and all was well – they would think that he and the others ought to be asked in.

So, after debating the matter for a few minutes they all rode off again. They wanted to get to Middlecombe Woods fairly soon, because there were no villages between Great Giddings and Middlecombe, so they would have to find the woods and then go on to find a farm-house somewhere to buy food for supper and breakfast. They hadn't been able to buy any in the shops at Great Giddings because it was early closing day, and they hadn't liked to ask the tea-shop woman to sell them anything. They felt they had taken quite enough of her food already!

They came to Middlecombe Woods, and found a very fine place to camp in for the night. It was in a little dell, set with primroses and violets, a perfectly hidden place, secure from all prying eyes, and surely unknown even to tramps.

'This is glorious,' said Anne. 'We must be miles away from anywhere: I hope we can find some farm-house or something that will sell us food, though! I know we don't feel hungry now, but we shall!'

'I think I've got a puncture, blow it,' said Dick, looking at his back tyre. 'It's a slow one, fortunately. But I think I won't risk coming along to look for farmhouses till I've mended it.'

'Right,' said Julian. 'And Anne needn't come either. She looks a bit tired. George and I will go. We won't take our bikes. It's easier to walk through the woods. We may be an hour or so, but don't worry, Timmy will know the way back all right, so we shan't lose you!'

Julian and George set off on foot, with Timmy following. Timmy too was tired, but nothing would have made him stay behind with Anne and Dick. He must go with his beloved George!

Anne put her bicycle carefully into the middle of a bush. You never knew when a tramp might be about, watching to steal something! It didn't matter when Timmy was there, because he would growl if a tramp came within a mile of them. Dick called out that he would mend his puncture now. He had found the hole already, where a small nail had gone in.

She sat near to Dick, watching him. She was glad to rest. She wondered if the others had found a farmhouse yet.

Dick worked steadily at mending the puncture. They had been there together about half an hour when they heard sounds.

Dick lifted his head and listened. 'Can you hear something?' he said to Anne. She nodded.

'Yes. Somebody's shouting. I wonder why!'

They both listened again. Then they distinctly heard yells. 'Help! Julian! Where are you? Help!'

They shot to their feet. Who was calling Julian for help? It wasn't George's voice. The yells grew louder, to panic-stricken shrieks.

'JULIAN! Dick!'

'Why – it must be Richard,' said Dick, amazed. 'What in the world does he want? What's happened?'

Anne was pale. She didn't like sudden happenings like this. 'Shall we – shall we go and find him?' she said.

There was a crashing not far off, as if somebody was making his way through the undergrowth. It was rather dark among the trees, and Anne and Dick could see nothing at first. Dick yelled loudly.

'Hey! Is that you, Richard! We're here!'

The crashing noise redoubled. 'I'm coming!' squealed Richard. 'Wait for me, wait for me!'

They waited. Soon they saw Richard coming, stumbling as fast as he could between the trees. 'Here we are,' called Dick. 'Whatever's the matter?'

Richard staggered towards them. He looked frightened out of his life. 'They're after me,' he panted. 'You must save me. I want Timmy. He'll bite them.'

'*Who*'s after you?' asked Dick, amazed.

'Where's Timmy? Where's Julian?' cried Richard, looking round in despair.

'They've gone to the farm-house to get some food,' said Dick. 'They'll be back soon, Richard. Whatever's the *matter*? Are you mad? You look awful.'

The boy took no notice of the questions. 'Where has

Julian gone? I want Timmy. Tell me the way they went. I can't stay here. They'll catch me!'

'They went along there,' said Dick, showing Richard the path. 'You can just see the tracks of their feet. Richard, whatever is . . .?'

But Richard was gone! He fled down the path at top speed, calling at the top of his voice, 'Julian! Timmy!'

Anne and Dick stared at one another in surprise. What had happened to Richard? Why wasn't he at his aunt's house? He must be mad!

'It's no good going after him,' said Dick. 'We shall only lose the way and not be able to find this place again – and the others will miss us and go hunting and get lost too! What *is* the matter with Richard?'

'He kept saying somebody was after him – *they* were after him!' said Anne. 'He's got some bee in his bonnet about something.'

'Bats in the belfry,' said Dick. 'Mad, dippy, daft! Well, he'll give Julian and George a shock when he runs into them – if he does! The odds are he will miss them altogether.'

'I'm going to climb this tree and see if I can see anything of Richard or the others,' said Anne. 'It's tall, and it's easy to climb. You finish mending your puncture. I should just love to know what happens to Richard.'

Dick went back to his bicycle, puzzled. Anne climbed the tree. She climbed well, and was soon at the top. She gazed out over the countryside. There was an expanse of fields on one side, and woods stretched away on the other. She looked over the darkening fields, trying to see if a farm-house was anywhere near. But she could see nothing.

Dick was just finishing his puncture when he heard another noise in the woods. Was it that idiot of a Richard coming back? He listened.

The noise came nearer. It wasn't a crashing noise, like

Richard had made. It was a stealthy noise as if people were gradually closing in. Dick didn't much like it. Who was coming? Or perhaps – *what* was coming? Was it some wild animal – perhaps a badger and its mate? The boy stood listening.

A silence came. No more movements. No more rustling. Had he imagined it all? He wished Anne and the others were near him. It was eerie, standing there in the darkening wood, waiting and watching.

He decided that he had imagined it all. He thought it would be a very good idea if he lighted his bicycle lamp, then the light would soon dispel his silly ideas! He fumbled about for it on the front of his handlebars. He switched it on and a very comforting little glow at once spread a circle of light in the little dell.

Dick was just about to call up to Anne to tell her his absurd fears when the noises came again! There was absolutely no mistake about them this time.

A brilliant light suddeningly pierced through the trees and fell on Dick. He blinked.

'Ah – so there you are, you little misery!' said a harsh voice, and someone came striding over to the dell. Somebody else followed behind.

'What do you mean?' asked Dick, amazed. He could not see who the men were because of the brilliant torch-light in his eyes.

'We've been chasing you for miles, haven't we? And you thought you'd get away. But we'd got you all the time!' said the voice.

'I don't understand this,' said Dick, putting on a bold voice. 'Who are you?'

'You know very well who we are,' said the voice. 'Didn't you run away screaming as soon as you saw Rooky? He went one way after you, and we went another – and we soon got you, didn't we? Now, you come along with us, my pretty!'

All this explained one thing clearly to Dick – that it was Richard they had been after, for some reason or other – and they thought *he* was Richard!

'I'm not the boy you're looking for,' he said. 'You'll get into trouble if you touch *me*!'

'What's your name, then?' asked the first man.

Dick told him.

'Oh – so you're Dick – and isn't Dick short for Richard? You can't fool us with that baby-talk,' said the first man. 'You're the Richard we want, all right. Richard Kent, see?'

'I'm *not* Richard Kent!' shouted Dick, as he felt the man's hand clutching his arm suddenly. 'You take your hands off me. You wait till the police hear of this!'

'They *won't* hear of it,' said the man. 'They won't hear anything at all! Come on – and don't struggle or shout or you'll be sorry. Once you're at Owl's Dene we'll deal properly with you!'

Anne was sitting absolutely petrified up in the tree. She couldn't move or speak. She tried to call out to poor Dick, but her tongue wouldn't say a word. She had to sit there and hear her brother being dragged away by two strange ruffians. She almost fell out of the tree in fright, and she heard him shouting and yelling when he was dragged away. She could hear the sound of crashing for a long time.

She began to cry. She didn't dare to climb down because she was trembling so much she was afraid she would lose her hold and fall.

She must wait for George and Julian to come back. Suppose they didn't? Suppose they had been caught too? She would be all by herself in the tree all night long. Anne sobbed up in the tree-top, holding on tightly.

The stars came out above her head, and she saw the very bright one again.

And then she heard the sound of footsteps and voices.

She stiffened up in the tree. Who was it this time? Oh let it be Julian and George and Timmy; let it be Julian, George and Timmy!

7

Richard tells a queer tale

Julian and George had managed to find a little farm-house tucked away in a hollow. A trio of dogs set up a terrific barking as they drew near. Timmy growled and the hair rose up on his neck. George put her hand on his collar.

'I won't go any nearer with Timmy,' she said. 'I don't want him to be set on by three dogs at once!'

So Julian went down to the farm-house by himself. The dogs made such a noise and looked so fierce that he paused in the farm-yard. He was not in the least afraid of dogs, but these looked most unpleasant, especially one big mongrel whose teeth were bared in a very threatening manner.

A voice called out to him. 'Clear off, you! We don't want no strangers here. When strangers come our eggs and hens go too!'

'Good evening,' called Julian, politely. 'We are four children camping out in the woods for the night. Could you let us have any food? I'll pay well for it.'

There was a pause. The man pulled his head in at the

window he was shouting from, and was evidently speaking to someone inside.

He stuck it out again. 'I told you, we don't hold with strangers here, never did. We've only got plain bread and butter, and we can give you some hardboiled eggs and milk and a bit of ham. That's all.'

'That'll do fine,' called Julian, cheerily. 'Just what we'd like. Shall I come and get it?'

'Not unless you want to be torn to pieces by them dogs,' came back the voice. 'You wait there. I'll be out when the eggs is done.'

'Blow,' said Julian, walking back to George. 'That means we'll have to kick our heels here for a while. What an unpleasant fellow! I don't think much of his place, do you!'

George agreed with him. It was ill-kept, the barn was falling to bits, rusty bits of machinery lay here and there in the thick grass. The three dogs kept up a continual barking and howling, but they did not come any nearer. George still kept her hand firmly on Timmy. He was bristling all over!

'What a lonely place to live in,' said Julian. 'No house within miles, I should think. No telephone. I wonder what they'd do if somebody was ill or had an accident and needed help.'

'I hope they'll hurry up with that food,' said George, getting impatient. 'It'll be dark soon. I'm getting hungry too.'

At last somebody came out of the tumble-down farmhouse. It was a bearded man, stooping and old, with long untidy hair and a pronounced limp. He had a grim and ugly face. Neither Julian nor George liked him.

'Here you are,' he said, waving his three dogs away behind him. 'Get back, you!' He aimed a kick at the nearest dog, and it yelped with pain.

'Oh don't!' said George. 'You hurt him.'

'He's my dog, ain't he?' said the man, angrily. 'You mind your own business!' He kicked out at another dog and scowled at George.

'What about the food?' said Julian, holding out his hand, anxious to be gone before trouble came between Timmy and the other dogs. 'George, take Timmy back a bit. He's upsetting the dogs.'

'Well, I like that!' said George. 'It's those other dogs that are upsetting *him*!'

She dragged Timmy back a few yards, and he stood there with all his hackles up on his neck, growling in a horrible way.

Julian took the food which was done up carelessly in old brown paper. 'Thanks,' he said. 'How much?'

'Five pounds,' said the old man, surprisingly.

'Don't be silly,' said Julian. He looked quickly at the food. 'I'll give you twenty-five pence for it, and that's more than it's worth. There's hardly any ham.'

'I said five pounds,' said the man, sullenly. Julian looked at him. 'He must be mad!' he thought. He held out the food to the ugly old fellow.

'Well, take it back,' he said. 'I haven't got five pounds to give you for food. Twenty-five pence is the most I can spare. Good night.'

The old man pushed the food back, and held out his other hand in silence. Julian fished in his pocket and brought out twenty-five pence. He placed them in the man's dirty hand, wondering why on earth the fellow had asked him for such a ridiculous sum before. The man put the money in his pocket.

'Clear off,' he said, suddenly, in a growling voice. 'We don't want strangers here, stealing our goods. I'll set my dogs on you if you come again!'

Julian turned to go, half-afraid that the extraordinary old man *would* set his dogs on him. The fellow stood there in the half-dark, yelling abuse at Julian and George as

they made their way out of the farm-yard.

'Well! We'll never go *there* again!' said George, furious at their treatment. 'He's mad as a hatter.'

'Yes. And I don't much fancy his food, either,' said Julian. 'Still, it's all we'll get tonight!'

They followed Timmy back to the woods. They were glad they had him, because otherwise they might have missed the way. But Timmy knew it. Once he had been along a certain route Timmy always knew it again. He ran on now, sniffing here and there, occasionally waiting for the others to catch him up.

Then he stiffened and growled softly. George put her hand on his collar. Somebody must be coming.

Somebody *was* coming! It was Richard on his way to find them. He was still shouting and yelling, and the noise he made had already come to Timmy's sharp ears. It soon came to Julian's, and George's too, as they stood there waiting.

'Julian! Where are you? Where's Timmy? I want Timmy! They're after me, I tell you; they're after me.'

'Listen – it sounds like *Richard*,' said Julian, startled. 'What in the world is he doing here? – and yelling like that too! Come on – we must find out. Something's happened. I hope Dick and Anne are all right.'

They ran up the path as fast as they could in the twilight. Soon they met Richard, who had now stopped shouting, and was stumbling along, half-sobbing.

'Richard! What's up?' cried Julian. Richard ran to him and flung himself against him. Timmy did not go to him, but stood there in surprise. George stared through the twilight, puzzled. What in the world had happened?

'Julian! Oh Julian! I'm scared stiff,' panted Richard, hanging on to Julian's arm.

'Pull yourself together,' said Julian, in the calm voice that had made a good effect on Richard. 'I bet you're just making a silly fuss. What's happened? Did you find your aunt was out or something? And come racing after us?'

'My aunt's away,' said Richard, speaking in a calmer voice. 'She . . .'

'*Away!*' said Julian, in surprise. 'But didn't your mother know that when she said you could . . .?'

'I didn't ask my mother's permission to come,' cried Richard. 'I didn't even go back home when you thought I did! I just biked straight to Croker's Corner and waited for you. I wanted to come with you, you see – and I knew my mother wouldn't let me.'

This was said with a great air of bravado. Julian was disgusted.

'I'm ashamed of you,' he said. 'Telling us lies like that!'

'I didn't know my aunt was away,' said Richard, all his sudden cockiness gone when he heard Julian's scornful voice. 'I thought she'd be there – and I was going to tell her to telephone my mother and say I'd gone for a trip with *you*. Then I thought I'd come biking after you and – and . . .'

'And tell us your aunt was away, and could you come with us?' finished Julian, still scornfully. 'A deceitful and ridiculous plan. I'd have sent you back at once; you might have known that.'

'Yes, I know. But I might have had a whole night camping out with you,' said Richard, in a small voice. 'I've never done things like that. I . . .'

'What I want to know is, what were you scared of when you came rushing along, yelling and crying,' said Julian, impatiently.

'Oh Julian – it was horrible,' said Richard, and he suddenly clutched Julian's arm again. 'You see – I biked down back to my aunt's gate – and out into the lane – and I was just going along the way to Middlecombe Woods when a car met me. And I saw who was in the car!'

'Well, *who*?' said Julian, feeling as if he could shake Richard.

'It was – it was Rooky!' said Richard, in a trembling voice.

'Who's he?' said Julian, and George gave an impatient click. Would Richard never tell his story properly?

'Don't you remember? – I told you about him. He was the fellow with thick lips and a huge nose that my father had for a bodyguard last year – and he chucked him out,' said Richard. 'He always swore he'd have his revenge on my father – and on me too because I told tales about him to Dad and it was because of that he was sacked. So when I caught sight of him in the car I was terrified!'

'I *see*,' said Julian, seeing light. 'What happened then?'

'Rooky recognized me, and turned the car round and chased me on my bike,' said Richard, beginning to tremble again as he remembered that alarming ride. 'I pedalled for all I was worth – and when I got to Middlecombe Woods I rode into the path there, hoping the car couldn't follow. It couldn't, of course – but the men leapt out – there were three of them, two I didn't know – and they chased me on foot. I pedalled and pedalled, and then I ran into a tree or something and fell off. I chucked my bike into a bush, and ran into the thick undergrowth to hide.'

'Go on,' said Julian, as Richard paused. 'What next?'

'The men split up then – Rooky went one way to find me, and the other two went another way. I waited till I thought they were gone, then I crept out and tore down the path again, hoping to find you. I wanted Timmy, you see, I thought he'd go for the men.'

Timmy growled. He certainly would have gone for them!

'Two of the men must have been hiding, waiting to hear me start up again,' went on Richard. 'And as soon as I began to run, they chased after me. I put them off the trail, though – I dodged and hid and hid and dodged – and then I came to Dick! He was mending a puncture. But you weren't with him – and it was you and Timmy I wanted – I knew the men would soon be catching me up, you see, so I tore on and on – and at last I found you. I've never been so glad in my life.'

It was a most extraordinary story – but Julian hardly paused to think about it. An alarming thought had come into his head. What about Dick and Anne? What would have happened to them if the men had suddenly come across them?

'Quick!' he said to George. 'We must get back to the others! Hurry!'

8

What's the best thing to do?

Stumbling through the dark wood, Julian and George hurried as best they could. Timmy hurried too, knowing that something was worrying both his friends. Richard followed behind, half-crying again. He really had been very much afraid.

They came at last to the little dell where they had planned to spend the night. It was quite dark. Julian called loudly:

'Dick! Anne! Where are you?'

George had made her way to where she had hidden her bicycle. She fumbled for the lamp and switched it on. She took it off and flashed it round the dell. There was Dick's bicycle, with the puncture repair outfit on the ground beside it – but no Dick, and no Anne! What had happened?

'Anne!' yelled Julian, in alarm. 'Dick! Come here! We're back!'

And then a small trembling voice came down from the tree-top overhead.

'Oh Julian! Oh Julian! I'm here.'

'It's Anne!' yelled Julian, his heart leaping in relief. 'Anne – where are you?'

'Up in this tree,' called back Anne, in a stronger voice. 'Oh Ju – I've been so frightened, I didn't dare climb down in case I fell. Dick . . .'

'Where *is* Dick?' demanded Julian.

A sob came down to him. 'Two horrible men came – and they've taken him away. They thought he was Richard!'

Anne's voice became a wail. Julian felt that he must get her down the tree so that she could be with them and be comforted. He spoke to George.

'Shine that lamp up here. I'm going up to fetch Anne.'

George silently shone the light of the lamp on the tree. Julian went up like a cat. He came to Anne who was still clinging tightly to a branch.

'Anne, I'll help you down. Come on, now – you can't fall. I'm just below you. I'll guide your feet to the right branches.'

Anne was only too glad to be helped down. She was cold and miserable, and she longed to be with the others. Slowly she came down, with Julian's help, and he lifted her to the ground.

She clung to him, and he put his arm round his young sister. 'It's all right, Anne. I'm with you now. And here's George too – and old Timmy.'

'Who's *that*?' said Anne, suddenly seeing Richard in the shadows.

'Only Richard. He's behaved badly,' said Julian, grimly. 'It's all because of him and his idiotic behaviour that this has happened. Now – tell us slowly and carefully about Dick and the two men, Anne.'

Anne told him, not missing out anything at all. Timmy stood near her, licking her hand all the time. That was very comforting indeed! Timmy always knew when any-

one was in trouble. Anne felt very much better when she had Julian's arm round her, and Timmy's tongue licking her!

'It's quite clear what's happened,' said Julian, when Anne had finished her alarming tale. 'This man Rooky recognized Richard, and he and the other two came after him, seeing a chance to kidnap him, and so get even with his father. Rooky was the only one who knew Richard, and he wasn't the man who caught Dick. The *others* got him – and they didn't know he wasn't Richard – and of course, hearing that his name was Dick they jumped to the conclusion that he was Richard – because Dick is short for Richard.'

'But Dick *told* them he wasn't Richard Kent,' said Anne, earnestly.

'Of course – but they thought he wasn't telling the truth,' said Julian. 'And they've taken him off. What did you say was the name of the place they were going to?'

'It sounded like Owl's Dene,' said Anne. 'Can we go there, Julian – if you told the men Dick was Dick and not Richard, they'd let him go, wouldn't they?'

'Oh yes,' said Julian. 'In any case, as soon as that fellow Rooky sets eyes on him he'll know there's a mistake been made. I think we can get old Dick away all right.'

A voice came out of the shadows nearby. 'What about *me*? Will you take me home first? *I* don't want to run into Rooky again.'

'I'm certainly not going to waste time taking *you* home,' said Julian, coldly. 'If it hadn't been for you and your tomfoolery we wouldn't have run into this trouble. You'll have to come with us. I'm going to find Dick first.'

'But I *can't* come with you – I'm afraid of Rooky!' wailed Richard.

'Well, stay here then,' said Julian, determined to teach Richard a lesson.

That was even worse. Richard howled loudly. 'Don't leave me here! Don't!'

'Now look here – if you come with us, you can always be dropped at a house somewhere, or at a police-station – and get yourself taken home somehow,' said Julian, exasperated. 'You're old enough to look after yourself. I'm fed up with you.'

Anne was sorry for Richard, although he had brought all this trouble on them. She knew how dreadful it was to feel really frightened. She put out a hand and touched him kindly.

'Richard! Don't be a baby. Julian will see that you're all right. He's just feeling cross with you now, but he'll soon get over it.'

'Don't you be too sure about that!' said Julian to Anne, pretending to be sterner than he really felt. 'What Richard wants is a jolly good hiding. He's untruthful and deceitful and an absolute baby!'

'Give me another chance,' almost wept poor Richard, who had never in his life been spoken to like this before. He tried to hate Julian for saying such things to him – but oddly enough he couldn't. He only respected and admired him all the more.

Julian said no more to Richard. He really thought the boy was too feeble for words. It was a nuisance that they had him with them. He would be no help at all – simply a tiresome nuisance.

'What are we going to do, Julian?' asked George, who had been very silent. She was fond of Dick, and was very worried about him. Where was Owl's Dene? How could they possibly find it in the night? And what about those awful men? How would they treat Julian if he demanded Dick back at once? Julian was fearless and straightforward – but the men wouldn't like him any the better for that.

'Well now – what *are* we going to do?' repeated Julian, and he fell silent.

'It's no good going back to that farm, and asking for help, is it?' said George, after a pause.

'Not a bit of good,' said Julian, at once. 'That old man wouldn't help anyone! And there's no telephone laid on, as we saw. No – that farm's no good. What a pity!'

'Where's the map?' said George, a sudden idea coming into her head. 'Would Owl's Dene be named on it, do you think?'

'Not if it's a house,' said Julian. 'Only places are named there. You'd want a frightfully big map to show every house.'

'Well, anyway – let's look at the map and see if it shows any more farms or villages,' said George, who felt as if she must *do* something, even if it was only looking at a map. Julian produced the map and unfolded it. He and the girls bent over it, by the light of the bicycle lamp, and Richard peered over their shoulders. Even Timmy tried to look, forcing his head under their arms.

'Get away, Tim,' said Julian. 'Look, here's where we are – Middlecombe Woods – see? My word, we *are* in a lonely spot! There's not a village for miles!'

Certainly no village was marked. The countryside was shown, hilly and wooded, with a stream here and there, and third-class roads now and again – but no village, no church, no bridge even was marked anywhere.

Anne gave a sudden exclamation and pointed to the contour of a hill on the map. 'Look – see what that hill's called?'

'Owl's Hill,' read out Julian. 'Yes – I see what you're getting at, Anne. If a house was built on that hill it might be called Owl's Dene, because of the name of the hill. What's more – a building *is* marked there! It hasn't a name, of course. It might be a farm-house, an old ruin – or a big house of some kind.'

'*I* think it's very likely that's where Owl's Dene is,' said George. 'I bet it's that very house. Let's take our bikes and go.'

A huge sigh from Richard attracted their attention. '*Now* what's the matter with you?' said Julian.

'Nothing. I'm hungry, that's all,' said Richard.

The others suddenly realized that they too were hungry. In fact, *terribly* hungry! It was a long, long time since tea.

Julian remembered the food he and George had brought from the farm. Should they have it now – or should they eat some on their way to Owl's Hill?

'Better eat as we go,' said Julian. 'Every minute we waste means a minute of worry for Dick.'

'I wonder what they'd do with him, if Rooky sees him and says he's not me, not the boy they want,' said Richard, suddenly.

'Set him free, I should think,' said George. 'Ruffians like that would probably turn him loose in a deserted countryside and not care tuppence if he found his way home or not. We've absolutely *got* to find out what's happened – whether he's at Owl's Dene, or been set free, or what.'

'I can't come with you,' suddenly wailed Richard.

'Why?' demanded Julian.

'Because I haven't got my bike,' said Richard, dolefully. 'I chucked it away, you remember – and goodness knows where it is. I'd never find it again.'

'He can have Dick's,' said Anne. 'There it is, over there – with the puncture mended too.'

'Oh yes,' said Richard, relieved. 'For one frightful moment I thought I'd have to be left behind.'

Julian secretly wished he *could* be left behind. Richard was more trouble than he was worth!

'Yes – you can take Dick's bike,' he said. 'But no idiotic behaviour with it, mind – no riding without handlebars, or any errand boy tricks like that. It's Dick's bike, not yours.'

Richard said nothing. Julian was always ticking him off. He supposed he deserved it – but it wasn't at all pleasant. He pulled at Dick's bike, and found the lamp was missing. Dick, of course, had taken it off. He hunted round for it and found it on the ground. Dick had let it fall, and the switch had turned itself off when the lamp hit the ground. When Richard pressed the switch down the lamp lighted again. Good!

'Now, come on,' said Julian, fetching his bicycle too. 'I'll hand out food to eat as we go. We must try to find our way to Owl's Hill as quick as ever we can!'

9

Moonlight adventure

The four of them rode carefully down the rough, woodland path. They were glad when they came out into a lane. Julian stopped for a moment to take his bearings.

'Now – according to the map, we ought to go to the right here – then take the left at the fork some way down, and then circle a hill by the road at the bottom – and then ride a mile or two in a little valley till we come to the foot of Owl's Hill.'

'If we meet anyone we could ask them about Owl's Dene,' said Anne, hopefully.

'We shan't meet anyone out at night in this district!' said Julian. 'For one thing it's far from any village, and there will be no farmer, no policeman, no traveller for miles! We can't hope to meet anyone.'

The moon was up, and the sky cleared as they rode down the lane. It was soon as bright as day!

'We could switch off our lamps and save the batteries,' said Julian. 'We can see quite well we're out of the woods and in the moonlight. Rather weird, isn't it?'

'I always think moonlight's queer, because although it shines so brightly on everything, you can never see much *colour* anywhere,' said Anne. She switched off her lamp too. She glanced down at Timmy.

'Switch off your head-lamps, Timmy!' she said, which made Richard give a sudden giggle. Julian smiled. It was nice to hear Anne being cheerful again.

'Timmy's eyes *are* rather like head-lamps, aren't they?' said Richard. 'I say – what about that food, Julian?'

'Right,' said Julian, and he fished in his basket. But it was very difficult to get it out with one hand, and try to hand it to the others.

'Better stop for a few minutes, after all,' he said at last. 'I've already dropped a hard-boiled egg, I think! Come on – let's stack our bikes by the side of the road for three minutes, and gulp down something just to satisfy us for now.'

Richard was only too pleased. The girls were so hungry that they too thought it a good idea. They leapt off their bicycles in the moonlit road and went to the little copse at the side. It was a pine-copse, and the ground below was littered with dry brown pine-needles.

'Let's squat here for a minute or two,' said Julian. 'I say – what's that over there?'

Everyone looked. 'It's a tumbledown hut or something,' said George, and she went nearer to see. 'Yes, that's all – some old cottage fallen to bits. There's only part of the walls left. Rather an eerie little place.'

They went to sit down under the pine-trees. Julian shared out the food. Timmy got his bit too, though not so much as he would have liked! They sat there in the pine shadows, munching hungrily as fast as they could.

'I say – can anyone hear what I hear?' said Julian, raising his head. 'It sounds like a car!'

They all listened. Julian was right. A car *was* purring silently through the countryside! What a bit of luck!

'If only it comes this way!' said Julian. 'We could stop it and ask it for help. It could take us to the nearest police-station at any rate!'

They left their food in the little copse and went to the roadside. They could see no head-lights shining anywhere, but they could still hear the noise of the car.

'Very quiet engine,' said Julian. 'Probably a powerful car. It hasn't got its head-lights on because of the bright moonlight.'

'It's coming nearer,' said George. 'It's coming down this lane. Yes – it is!'

So it was. The noise of the engine came nearer, and nearer. The children got ready to leap out into the road to stop the car.

And then the noise of the engine died away suddenly. The moon shone down on a big streamlined car that had stopped a little way down the lane. It had no lights at all, not even side-lights. Julian put out his hand to stop the others from rushing into the road and shouting.

'Wait,' he said. 'This is just a bit – queer!'

They waited, keeping in the shadows. The car had stopped not far from the tumbledown hut. A door opened on the off-side. A man got out and rushed across the road to the shadow of the hedge there. He seemed to be carrying a bundle of some kind.

A low whistle sounded. The call of an owl came back. 'An answering signal!' thought Julian, intensely curious about all this. 'I wonder what's happening?'

'Keep absolutely quiet,' he breathed to the others. 'George, look after Timmy – don't let him growl.'

But Timmy knew when he had to be quiet. He didn't even give a whine. He stood like a statue, ears pricked, eyes watching the lane.

Nothing happened for a while. Julian moved very cautiously to the shelter of another tree, from where he could see better.

He could see the tumbledown shack. He saw a shadow moving towards it from some trees beyond. He saw a man waiting – the man from the car probably. Who were they? What in the world could they be doing here at this time of night?

The man from the trees came at last to the man from the car. There was a rapid interchange of words, but Julian could not hear what they were. He was sure that the men had no idea at all that he and the other children were near. He cautiously crept to yet another tree, and peered from the shadows to try and see what was happening.

'Don't be long,' he heard one man say. 'Don't bring your things to the car. Stuff them down the well.'

Julian could not see properly what the man was doing, but he thought he must be changing his clothes. Yes – now he was putting on the others – probably from the bundle the first man had brought from the car. Julian was more and more curious. What a queer business! Who was the second man? A refugee? A spy?

The man who had changed his clothes now picked up his discarded ones and went to the back of the shack. He came back without them, and followed the first man across the lane to the waiting car.

Even before the door had closed, the engine was purring, and the car was away! It passed by the pine-copse where the children were watching, and they all shrank back as it raced by. Before it had gone very far it was travelling very fast indeed.

Julian joined the others. Well – what do you make of all that?' he said. 'Funny business, isn't it? I watched a man changing his clothes – goodness knows why. He's left them somewhere at the back of the shack – down a well, I think I heard them say. Shall we see?'

'Yes, let's,' said George, puzzled. 'I say, did you see the number on the car. I only managed to spot the letters – KMF.'

'I saw the numbers,' said Anne. '102. And it was a black Bentley.'

'Yes. Black Bentley, KMF 102,' said Richard. 'Up to some funny business, I'll be bound!'

They made their way to the ruined shack, and pushed through overgrown weeds and bushes into the backyard. There was a broken-down well there, most of its brick-work missing.

It was covered by an old wooden lid. Julian removed it. It was still heavy, though rotten with age. He peered down the well, but there was nothing at all to be seen. It was far too deep to see to the bottom by the light of a bicycle lamp.

'Not much to be seen *there*,' said Julian, replacing the lid. 'I expect it *was* his clothes he threw down. Wonder why he changed them?'

'Do you think he could be an escaped prisoner?' said Anne, suddenly. 'He'd have to change his prison clothes, wouldn't he? – that would be the most important thing for him to do. Is there a prison near here?'

Nobody knew. 'Don't remember noticing one on the map,' said Julian. 'No – somehow I don't think the man was an escaped prisoner – more likely a spy dropped down in this desolate countryside, and supplied with clothes – or perhaps a deserter from the army. That's even *more* likely!'

'Well, whatever it is I don't like it and I'm jolly glad the car's gone with the prisoner or deserter or spy, whatever he is,' said Anne. 'What a curious thing that we should just be nearby when this happened! The men would never, never guess there were four children and a dog watching just a few yards away.'

'Lucky for us they *didn't* know,' said Julian. 'They wouldn't have been at all pleased! Now come on – we've wasted enough time. Let's get back to our food. I hope Timmy hasn't eaten it all. We left it on the ground.'

Timmy hadn't eaten even a crumb. He was sitting

patiently by the food, occasionally sniffing at it. All that bread and ham and eggs waiting there and nobody to eat it!

'Good dog,' said George. 'You're very, very trustable, Timmy. You shall have a big bit of bread and ham for your reward.'

Timmy gulped it down in one mouthful, but there was no more for him to have. The others only just had enough for themselves, and ate every crumb. They rose to their feet in a very few minutes and went to get their bicycles.

'Now for Owl's Hill again,' Julian. 'And let's hope we don't come across any more queer happenings tonight. We've had quite enough.'

10

Owl's Dene on Owl's Hill

Off they went again, cycling fast in the brilliant moon-light. Even when the moon went behind a cloud it was still light enough to ride without lights. They rode for what seemed like miles, and then came to a steep hill.

'Is this Owl's Hill?' said Anne, as they dismounted to walk up it. It was too steep to ride.

'Yes,' said Julian. 'At least, I think so – unless we've come quite wrong. But I don't think we have. Now the thing is – shall we find Owl's Dene at the top or not? And how shall we know it *is* Owl's Dene!'

'We could ring the bell and ask,' said Anne.

Julian laughed. That was so like Anne. 'Maybe we'll have to do that!' he said. 'But we'll scout round a bit first.'

They pushed their bicycles up the steep road. Hedges bordered each side, and fields lay beyond. There were no animals in them that the children could see – no horses, sheep or cows.

'Look!' said Anne, suddenly. 'I can see a building – at least, I'm sure I can see chimneys!'

They looked where she pointed. Yes – certainly they were chimneys – tall, brick chimneys that looked old.

'Looks like an Elizabethan mansion, with chimneys like that,' said Julian. He paused and took a good look. 'It must be a big place. We ought to come to a drive or something soon.'

They pushed on with their bicycles. Gradually the house came into view. It was more like a mansion, and in the moonlight it looked old, rather grand and very beautiful.

'There are the gates,' said Julian, thankfully. He was

tired of pushing his bicycle up the hill. 'They're shut. Hope they're not locked!'

As they drew near to the great, wrought-iron gates, they slowly opened. The children paused in surprise. Why were they opening? Not for them, that was certain!

Then they heard the sound of a car in the distance. Of course, that was what the gates were opening for. The car, however, was not coming up the hill – it was coming down the drive on the other side of the gates.

'Get out of sight, quickly,' said Julian. 'We don't want to be seen yet.'

They crouched down in the ditch with their bicycles as a car came slowly out of the open gates. Julian gave an exclamation and nudged George.

'See that? It's the black Bentley again – KMF 102!'

'How mysterious!' said George, surprised. 'What's it doing rushing about the country at night and picking up stray men! Taking them to this place too. I wonder if it *is* Owl's Dene.'

The car went by and disappeared round a bend in the hill. The children came out of the ditch with Timmy and their bicycles.

'Let's walk cautiously up to the gates,' said Julian. 'They're still open. Funny how they opened when the car came. I never saw anyone by them!'

They walked boldly up to the open gates.

'Look!' said Julian, pointing up to the great brick posts from which the gates were hung. They all looked, and exclaimed at the name shining there.

'Well! So it *is* Owl's Dene, after all!'

'There's the name in brass letters – Owl's Dene! We've found it!'

'Come on,' said Julian, wheeling his bicycle through the gateway. 'We'll go in and snoop round. We might be lucky enough to find old Dick somewhere about.'

They all went through the gates – and then Anne clutched Julian in fright. She pointed silently behind them.

The gates were closing again! But nobody was there to shut them. They closed silently and smoothly all by themselves. There was something very weird about that.

'Who's shutting them?' whispered Anne, in a scared voice.

'I think it must be done by machinery,' whispered back Julian. 'Probably worked from the house. Let's go back and see if we can find any machinery that works them.'

They left their bicycles by the side of the drive and walked back to the gates. Julian looked for a handle or latch to open them. But there was none.

He pulled at the gates. They did not budge. It was quite impossible to open them. They had been shut and locked by some kind of machinery, and nothing and nobody could open them but that special machinery.

'Blow!' said Julian, and he sounded so angry that the others looked at him in surprise.

'Well, don't you see? – we're locked in! We're as much prisoners here as Dick is, if he's here too. We can't get out through the gates – and if you take a look you'll see a high wall running round the property from the gates – and I don't mind betting it goes the *whole* way round. We can't get out even if we want to.'

They went back thoughtfully to their bicycles. 'Better wheel them a little way into the trees and leave them,' said Julian. 'They hinder us too much now. We'll leave them and go snooping quietly round the house. Hope there are no dogs.'

They left their bicycles well hidden among the trees at the side of the wide drive. The drive was not at all well-kept. It was mossy and weeds grew all over it. It was bare only where the wheels of cars had passed.

'Shall we walk up the drive or keep to the side?' asked George.

'Keep to the side,' said Julian. 'We should easily be seen in the moonlight, walking up the drive.'

So they kept to the side, in the shadows of the trees. They followed the curves of the long drive until the house itself came into sight.

It really was very big indeed. It was built in the shape of the letter E with the middle stroke missing – E. There was a courtyard in front, overgrown with weeds. A low wall, about knee high, ran round the courtyard.

There was a light in a room on the top floor, and another one on the ground floor. Otherwise from that side the house was dark.

'Let's walk quietly round it,' said Julian, in a low voice. 'Goodness – what's that?'

It was a weird and terrible screech that made them all jump in alarm. Anne clutched Julian in fright.

They stood and listened.

Something came down silently and brushed George's hair. She almost screamed – but before she could, that terrible screech came again, and she put out her hand to quieten Timmy, who was amazed and scared.

'What is it, Ju!' whispered George. 'Something touched me then. Before I could see what it was it was gone.'

'Listen – it's all right,' whispered back Julian. 'It's only an owl – a screech owl!'

'Good gracious – so it was,' breathed back George, in great relief. 'What an ass I was not to think of it. It's a barn-owl – a screech owl out hunting. Anne, were you scared?'

'I should just think I was!' said Anne, letting go her hold on Julian's arm.

'So was I,' said Richard, whose teeth were still chattering with fear. 'I nearly ran for my life! I would have too, if I could have got my legs to work – but they were glued to the ground!'

The owl screeched again, a little farther away, and another one answered it. A third one screeched, and the night was really made hideous with the unearthly calls.

'I'd rather have a brown owl any day, calling To-whooo-oo-oo,' said George. 'That's a nice noise. But this screeching is frightful.'

'No wonder it's called Owl's Hill,' said Julian. 'Perhaps it's always been a haunt of the screech-owls.'

The four children and Timmy began to walk quietly round the house, keeping to the shadows as much as they could. Everywhere was dark at the back except two long windows. They were leaded windows, and curtains were pulled across them. Julian tried to see through the cracks.

He found a place where two curtains didn't quite meet. He put his eye to the crack and looked in.

'It's the kitchen,' he told the others. 'An enormous place – lighted with one big oil-lamp. All the rest of the room is in shadow. There's a great fire-place at the end, with a few logs burning in it.'

'Anyone there?' asked George, trying to see through the

crack too. Julian moved aside and let her take her turn.

'No one that I can see,' he said. George gave an exclamation as she looked, and Julian pushed her aside to look in again.

He saw a man walking into the room – a queer, dwarf-like fellow, with a hunched back that seemed to force his head on one side. He had a very evil face. Behind him came a woman – thin, drab and the picture of misery.

The man flung himself into a chair and began to fill a pipe. The woman took a kettle off the fire and went to fill hot-water bottles in a corner.

'She must be the cook,' thought Julian. 'What a misery she looks! I wonder what the man is – man-of-all-work, I suppose. What an evil face he's got!'

The woman spoke timidly to the man in the chair. Julian, of course, could not hear a word from outside the window. The man answered her roughly, banging on the arm of the chair as he spoke.

The woman seemed to be pleading with him about something. The man flew into a rage, picked up a poker and threatened the woman with it. Julian watched in horror. Poor woman! No wonder she looked miserable if that was the sort of thing that kept happening.

However, the man did nothing with the poker except brandish it in temper, and he soon replaced it, and settled down in his chair again. The woman said no more at all, but went on filling the bottles. Julian wondered who they were for.

He told the others what he had seen. They didn't like it at all. If the people in the kitchen behaved like that whatever would those in the other part of the house be like?

They left the kitchen windows and went on round the house. They came to a lower room, lighted inside. But here the curtains were tightly drawn, and there was no crack to look through.

They looked up to the one room high up that was lighted. Surely Dick must be there? Perhaps he was locked up in the attic, all by himself? How they wished they knew!

Dared they throw up a stone? They wondered if they should try. There didn't seem any way at all of getting into the house. The front door was well and truly shut. There was a side door also tightly shut and locked, because they had tried it. Not a single window seemed to be open.

'I think I *will* throw up a stone,' said Julian at last. 'I feel sure Dick's up there, if he has been taken here – and you're certain you heard the men say "Owl's Dene", aren't you, Anne?'

'Quite certain,' said Anne. 'Do throw a stone, Julian. I'm getting so worried about poor Dick.'

Julian felt about on the ground for a stone. He found one embedded in the moss that was everywhere. He balanced it in his hand. Then up went the stone, but fell just short of the window. Julian got another. Up it went – and hit the glass of the window with a sharp crack. Somebody came to the pane at once.

Was it Dick? Everyone strained their eyes to see – but the window was too far up. Julian threw up another stone, and that hit the window too.

'I think it *is* Dick,' said Anne. 'Oh dear – no it isn't after all. Can't *you* see, Julian?'

But the person at the window, whoever he was, had now disappeared. The children felt a bit uncomfortable. Suppose it hadn't been Dick? Suppose it had been someone else who had now disappeared from the room to go and look for them?

'Let's get away from this part of the house,' whispered Julian. 'Get round to the other side.'

They made their way round quietly – and Richard suddenly pulled at Julian's arm. 'Look!' he said. 'There's a window open! Can't we get in there?'

11

Trapped!

Julian looked at the casement window. The moonlight shone on it. It certainly was a little ajar. 'How did we miss that when we went round before?' he wondered. He hesitated a little. Should they try to get in or not? Wouldn't it be better to rap on the back door and get that miserable-looking woman to answer it and tell them what they wanted to know?

On the other hand there was that evil-looking hunchback there. Julian didn't like the look of him at all. No – on the whole it might be better to creep in at the window, see if it was Dick upstairs, set him free, and then all escape through the same open window. Nobody would know. The bird would have flown, and everything would be all right.

Julian went to the window. He put a leg up and there he was astride the window. He held out a hand to Anne. 'Come on – I'll give you a hand,' he said, and pulled her up beside him. He lifted her down on the floor inside.

Then George came, and then Richard. George was just

leaning out to encourage Timmy to jump in through the window too, when something happened!

A powerful torchlight went on, and its beam shone right across the room into the dazzled eyes of the four children! They stood there, blinking in alarm. What was this?

Then Anne heard the voice of one of the men who had captured Dick, 'Well, well, well – a crowd of young burglars!'

The voice changed suddenly to anger. 'How *dare* you break in here! I'll hand you over to the police.'

From outside Timmy growled fiercely. He jumped up at the window and almost succeeded in leaping through. The man grasped what was happening at once, and went to the open window. He shut it with a bang. Now Timmy couldn't get in!

'Let my dog in!' said George, angrily, and stupidly tried to open the window again. The man brought his torch down sharply on her hand and she cried out in pain.

'That's what happens to boys who go against my wishes,' said the man, whilst poor George nursed her bruised hand.

'Look here,' began Julian, fiercely, 'what do you think you're doing? We're not burglars – and what's more we'd be very, very glad if you'd hand us over to the police!'

'Oh, you would, would you?' said the man. He went to the door of the room and yelled out in a tremendous voice: 'Aggie! AGGIE! Bring a lamp here at once.'

There was an answering shout from the kitchen, and almost immediately the light of a lamp appeared shining down the passage outside. It grew brighter, and the miserable-looking woman came in with a big oil-lamp. She stared in amazement at the little group of children. She seemed about to say something when the man gave her a rough push.

'Get out. And keep your mouth shut. Do you hear me?'

The woman scuttled out like a frightened hen. The man looked round at the children in the light of the lamp. The room was very barely furnished and appeared to be a sitting-room of some kind.

'So you don't mind being given up to the police?' said the man. 'That's very interesting. You think they'd approve of you breaking into my house?'

'I tell you, we *didn't* break in,' said Julian, determined to get that clear, at any rate. 'We came here because we had reason to believe that you've got my brother locked up somewhere in this house – and it's all a mistake. You've got the wrong boy.'

Richard didn't like this at all. He was terribly afraid of being locked up in the place of Dick! He kept behind the others as much as possible.

The man looked hard at Julian. He seemed to be

thinking. 'We haven't a boy here at all,' he said at last. 'I really don't know what you mean. You don't suggest that I go about the countryside picking boys up and making them prisoners, do you?'

'I don't know what you do,' said Julian. 'All I know is this – you captured Dick, my brother, this evening in Middlecombe Woods – thinking he was Richard Kent – well, he's not, he's my brother Dick. And if you don't set him free at once, I'll tell the police what we know.'

'And dear me – *how* do you know all this?' asked the man. 'Were you there when he was captured, as you call it?'

'One of us was,' said Julian, bluntly. 'In the tree overhead. That's how we know.'

There was a silence. The man took out a cigarette and lighted it. 'Well, you're quite mistaken,' he said. 'We've no boy held prisoner here. The thing is ridiculous. Now it's very, very late – would you like to bed down here for the night and get off in the morning? I don't like to send a parcel of kids out into the middle of the night. There's no telephone here, or I'd ring your home.'

Julian hesitated. He felt certain Dick was in the house. If he said he would stay for the night he might be able to find out if Dick was really there or not. He could quite well see that the man didn't want them tearing off to the police. There was something at Owl's Dene that was secret and sinister.

'I'll stay,' he said at last. 'Our people are away – they won't worry.'

He had forgotten about Richard for the moment. His people certainly *would* worry! Still, there was nothing to do about it. The first thing was to find Dick. Surely the men would be mad to hold him a prisoner once they were certain he wasn't the boy. Perhaps Rooky, the ruffian who knew Richard, hadn't yet arrived – hadn't seen Dick? That must be the reason that this man wanted them to stay the night. Of course – he'd wait till Rooky came – and when Rooky said, 'No – he's not the boy we want!' they'd let Dick go. They'd have to!

The man called for Aggie again. She came at once.

'These kids are lost,' said the man to her. 'I've said I'll put them up for the night. Get one of the rooms ready – just put down mattresses and blankets – that's all. Give them some food if they want it.'

Aggie was evidently tremendously astonished. Julian guessed that she was not used to this man being kind to lost children. He shouted at her.

'Well, don't stand dithering there. Get on with the job. Take these kids with you.'

Aggie beckoned to the four children. George hung back. 'What about my dog?' she said. 'He's still outside, whining. I can't go to bed without him.'

'You'll have to,' said the man, roughly. 'I won't have him in the house at any price, and that's flat.'

'He'll attack anyone he meets,' said George.

'He won't meet anyone out there,' said the man. 'By the way – how did you get in through the gates?'

'A car came out just as we got there and we slipped in before the gates closed,' said Julian. 'How do the gates shut? By machinery?'

'Mind your own business,' said the man, and went down the passage in the opposite direction.

'Pleasant, kindly fellow,' said Julian to George.

'Oh, a sweet nature,' answered George. The woman stared at them both in surprise. She didn't seem to realize that they meant the opposite to what they said! She led the way upstairs.

She came to a big room with a carpet on the floor, a small bed in a corner, and one or two chairs. There was no other furniture.

'I'll get some mattresses and put them down for you,' she said.

'I'll help you,' offered Julian, thinking it would be a good idea to see round a bit.

'All right,' said the woman. 'You others stay here.'

She went off with Julian. They went to a cupboard and the woman tugged at two big mattresses. Julian helped her. She seemed rather touched by this help.

'Well, thank you,' she said. 'They're pretty heavy.'

'Don't expect you have many children here, to stay, do you?' asked Julian.

'Well, it's funny that you should come just after . . .' the woman began. Then she stopped and bit her lip, looking anxiously up and down the passage.

'Just after what?' asked Julian. 'Just after the other boy came, do you mean?'

'Sh!' said the woman, looking scared to death. 'Whatever do you know about *that*? You shouldn't have said that. Mr Perton will skin me alive if he knew you'd said that. He'd be sure I'd told you. Forget about it.'

'That's the boy who's locked up in one of the attics at the top of the house isn't it?' said Julian, helping her to carry one of the mattresses to the big bedroom. She dropped her end in the greatest alarm.

'Now! Do you want to get me into terrible trouble – and yourselves too? Do you want Mr. Perton to tell old Hunchy to whip you all? You don't know that man! He's wicked.'

'When's Rooky coming?' asked Julian, bent on astonishing the woman, hoping to scare her into one admission after another. This was too much for her altogether. She stood there shaking at the knees, staring at Julian as if she couldn't believe her ears.

'What do you know about Rooky?' she whispered. 'Is he coming here? Don't tell me he's coming here!'

'Why? Don't you like him?' asked Julian. He put a hand on her shoulder. 'Why are you so frightened and upset? What's the matter? Tell me. I might be able to help you.'

'Rooky's bad,' said the woman. 'I thought he was in prison. Don't tell me he's out again. Don't tell me he's coming here.'

She was so frightened that she wouldn't say a word more. She began to cry, and Julian hadn't the heart to press her with any more questions. In silence he helped her to drag the mattresses into the other room.

'I'll get you some food,' said the poor woman, sniffing miserably. 'You'll find blankets in that cupboard over there if you want to lie down.'

She disappeared. Julian told the others in whispers what he had been able to find out. 'We'll see if we can find

Dick as soon as things are quiet in the house,' he said. 'This is a bad house – a house of secrets, of queer comings and goings. I shall slip out of our room and see what I can find out later on. I think that man – Mr Perton is his name – is really waiting for Rooky to come and see if Dick is Richard or not. When he finds he isn't I've no doubt he'll set him free – and us too.'

'What about *me*?' said Richard. 'Once he sees me, I'm done for. I'm the boy he wants. He hates my father and he hates me too. He'll kidnap me, take me somewhere, and ask an enormous ransom for me – just to punish us!'

'Well, we must do something to prevent him seeing you,' said Julian. 'But I don't see why he *should* see you – it's only Dick he'll want to see. He won't be interested in what he thinks are Dick's brothers and sisters! Now for goodness' sake don't start to howl again, or honestly I'll give you up to Rooky myself! You really are a frightful little coward – haven't you any courage at all!'

'All this has come about because of your silly lies and deceit,' said George, quiet fiercely. 'It's all because of you that our trip is spoilt, that Dick's locked up – and poor Timmy's outside without me.'

Richard looked quite taken aback. He shrank into a corner and didn't say another word. He was very miserable. Nobody liked him – nobody believed him – nobody trusted him. Richard felt very, very small indeed.

12

Julian looks round

The woman brought them some food. It was only bread and butter and jam, with some hot coffee to drink. The four children were not really hungry, but they were very thirsty, and they drank the coffee eagerly.

George opened the window and called softly down to Timmy. 'Tim! Here's something for you!'

Timmy was down there all right, watching and waiting. He knew where George was. He had howled and whined for some time, but now he was quiet.

George was quite determined to get him indoors if she could. She gave him all her bread and jam, dropping it down bit by bit, and listening to him wolfing it up. Anyway, old Timmy would know she was thinking of him!

'Listen,' said Julian, coming in from the passage outside, where he had stood listening for a while. 'I think it would be a good idea if we put out this light, and settled down on the mattresses. But I shall make up a lump on mine to look like me, so that if anyone comes they'll think I'm there on the mattress. But I shan't be.'

'Where will you be, then?' asked Anne. 'Don't leave us!'

'I shall be hiding outside in that cupboard,' said Julian. 'I've a sort of feeling that our pleasant host, Mr Perton, will come along presently to lock us in – and I've no intention of being locked in! I think he'll flash a torch into the room, see that we're all four safely asleep on the mattresses, and then quietly lock the door. Well – *I* shall be able to unlock it when I come back from the cupboard outside – and we shan't be prisoners at all!'

'Oh – that really is a good idea,' said Anne, cuddling herself up in a blanket. 'You'd better go and get into the cupboard now, Julian, before we're locked up for the night!'

Julian blew out the lamp. He tiptoed to the door and opened it. He left it ajar. He went into the passage and fumbled his way to where he knew the cupboard should be. Ah – there it was. He pulled at the handle and the door opened silently. He slipped inside and left the door open just a crack, so that he would be able to see if anyone came along the wide passage.

He waited there about twenty minutes. The cupboard smelt musty, and it was very boring standing there doing absolutely nothing.

Then, through the crack in the door, he suddenly noticed that a light was coming. Ah – somebody was about!

He peered through the crack. He saw Mr Perton coming quietly along the corridor with a little oil-lamp held in his hand. He went to the door of the children's bedroom and pushed it a little. Julian watched him, hardly daring to breathe.

Would he notice that the figure on one of the mattresses was only a lump made of a blanket rolled up and covered by another blanket? Julian fervently hoped that he wouldn't. All his plans would be spoilt if so.

Mr Perton held the lamp high in his hand and looked

cautiously into the room. He saw four huddled-up shapes lying on the mattresses – four children – he thought.

They were obviously asleep. Softly, Mr Perton closed the door, and just as softly locked it. Julian watched anxiously to see if he pocketed the key or not. No – he hadn't! He had left it in the lock. Oh good!

The man went away again, treading softly. He did not go downstairs, but disappeared into a room some way down on the right. Julian heard the door shut with a click. Then he heard another click. The man evidently believed in locking himself in. Perhaps he didn't trust his other comrade, wherever he was – or Hunchy or the woman.

Julian waited a while and then crept out of the cupboard. He stole up to Mr Perton's room and looked through the keyhole to see if the room was in darkness or not. It was! Was Mr Perton snoring? Not that Julian could hear.

However Julian was not going to wait till he heard Mr Perton snore. He was going to find Dick – and he was pretty certain that the first place to look was in that attic upstairs!

'I bet Mr Perton was up there with Dick and heard me throwing stones at the window,' thought Julian. 'Then he slipped down and opened that window to trap us into getting in there – and we fell neatly into the trap! He must have been waiting inside the room for us. I don't like Mr Perton – too full of bright ideas!'

He was half-way up the flight of stairs that led to the attics now – going very carefully and slowly, afraid of making the stairs creak loudly. They did creak – and at every creak poor Julian stopped and listened to see if anyone had heard!

There was a long passage at the top turning at both ends into the side-wings. Julian stood still and debated – now which way ought he to go? – where exactly was that lighted window? It was somewhere along this long passage, he was certain. Well, he'd go along the doors and see if a light shone out through the keyhole, or under the door anywhere.

Door after door was ajar. Julian peeped round each, making out bare dark attics, or box-rooms with rubbish in. Then he came to a door that was closed. He peered through the keyhole. No light came from inside the room.

Julian knocked gently. A voice came at once – Dick's voice. 'Who's there?'

'Sh! It's me – Julian,' whispered Julian. 'Are you all right, Dick?'

There came the creak of a bed, then the pattering of feet across a bare floor. Dick's voice came through the door, muffled and cautious.

'Julian! How did you get here? This is marvellous! Can you unlock the door and let me out?'

Julian had already felt for a key – but there was none. Mr Perton had taken *that* key, at any rate!

'No. The key's gone,' he said. 'Dick, what did they do to you?'

'Nothing much. They dragged me off to the car and shoved me in,' said Dick, through the door. 'The man called Rooky wasn't there. The others waited for him for some time, then drove off. They thought he might have gone off to see someone they meant to visit. So I haven't seen him. He's coming tomorrow morning. What a shock for him when he finds I'm not Richard!'

'Richard's here too,' whispered Julian. 'I wish he wasn't – because if Rooky happens to see him he'll be kidnapped, I'm sure! The only hope is that Rooky will only see *you* – and as the other men think we're all one family, they may let us all go. Did you come straight here in the car, Dick?'

'Yes,' said Dick. 'The gates opened like magic when we got here, but I couldn't see anybody. I was shoved up here and locked in. One of the men came to tell me all the things

Rooky was going to do to me when he saw me – and then he suddenly went downstairs and hasn't come back again.'

'Oh – I bet that was when we chucked stones up at your window,' said Julian at once. 'Didn't you hear them?'

'Yes – so that was the crack I heard! The man with me went across to the window at once – and he must have seen you. Now, what about *you*, Ju? How on earth did you get here? are you all really here? I suppose that was Timmy I heard howling outside.'

Julian quickly told him all his tale from the time he and George had met the howling Richard to the moment he had slipped up the stairs to find Dick.

There was a silence when he had finished his tale. Then Dick's voice came through the crack.

'Not much good making any plans, Julian. If things go all right, we'll be out of here by the morning, when Rooky finds I'm not the boy he wants. If things go wrong at least we're all together, and we can make plans then. I wonder what his mother will think when Richard doesn't get home tonight.'

'Probably think he's gone off to the aunt's,' said Julian. 'I should think he's a very unreliable person. Blow him! It was all because of him we got into this fix.'

'I expect the men will have some cock-and-bull story tomorrow morning, about why they got hold of you, when they find you're not Richard,' went on Julian. 'They'll probably say you threw stones at their car or something, and they took you in hand – or found your hurt and brought you here to help you! Anyway, whatever they say, we won't make much fuss about it. We'll go quietly – and then we'll get things moving! I don't know what's going on here, but it's something queer. The police ought to look into it, I'm certain.'

'Listen – that's Timmy again,' said Dick. 'Howling like anything for George, I suppose. You'd better go,

Julian, in case he wakes up one of the men and they come out and find you here. Good-night. I'm awfully glad you're near! Thanks awfully for coming to find me.'

'Good-night,' said Julian, and went back along the corridor, walking over the patches of moonlight, looking fearfully into the dark shadows in case Mr Perton or somebody else was waiting for him!

But nobody was about. Timmy's howling died down. There was a deep silence in the house. Julian went down the stairs to the floor on which the bedroom was where the others lay asleep. He paused outside it. Should he do any further exploring? It really was such a chance!

He decided that he would. Mr Perton was fast asleep, he hoped. He thought probably Hunchy and the woman had gone to bed too. He wondered where the other man was, who had brought Dick to Owl's Dene. He hadn't seen him at all. Perhaps he had gone out in that black Bentley they had seen going out of the gate.

Julian went down to the ground floor. A brilliant thought had just occurred to him. Couldn't he undo the front door and get the others down, and send them out, free? He himself couldn't escape, because it would mean leaving Dick alone.

Then he gave up the idea. 'No,' he thought. 'For one thing George and Anne would refuse to go without me – and even if they agreed to get out of the front door, and go down the drive to the gates, how would they undo them? They're worked by some machinery from the house.'

So his brilliant idea came to nothing. He decided to look into all the rooms on the ground floor. He looked into the kitchen first. The fire was almost out. The moonlight came through the cracks of the curtains and lighted up the dark silent room. Hunchy and the woman had evidently retired somewhere.

There was nothing of interest in the kitchen. Julian went into the room opposite. It was a dining-room, with a

long polished table, candlesticks on the walls and mantelpiece, and the remains of a wood fire. Nothing of interest
there either.

The boy went into another room. Was it a workroom, or
what? There was a radiogram there, and a big desk. There
was a stand with a curious instrument of some kind that
had a stout wheel-like handle. Julian suddenly wondered
if it would open the gates! Yes – that was what it was for.
He saw a label attached to it. Left Gate. Right Gate. Both
Gates.

'That's what it is – the machinery for opening either or
both of the gates. If only I could get Dick out of that room
I'd get us all out of this place in no time!' said Julian. He
twisted the handle – what would happen?

13

Strange secret

A curious groaning, whining noise began, as some kind of strong machinery was set working. Julian hurriedly turned the handle back. If it was going to make all that noise, he wasn't going to try his hand at opening the gates! It would bring Mr Perton out of his room in a rush!

'Most ingenious, whatever it is,' thought the boy, examining it as well as he could in the moonlight that streamed through the window. He looked round the room again. A noise came to his ears and he stood still.

'It's somebody snoring,' he thought. 'I'd better not mess about here any more! Where are they sleeping? Somewhere not far from here, that's certain.'

He tiptoed cautiously into the next room and looked inside it. It was a lounge, but there was nobody there at all. He couldn't hear the snoring there either.

He was puzzled. There didn't seem to be any other room nearby where people could sleep. He went back to the workroom or study. Yes – now he could hear that noise again – and it *was* somebody snoring! Somebody quite near – and yet not near enough to hear properly, or to see. Most peculiar.

Julian walked softly round the room, trying to find a place where the snoring sounded loudest of all. Yes – by this bookcase that reached to the ceiling. That was where the snoring sounded most of all. Was there a room behind this wall, next to the workroom? Julian went out to investigate. But there was no room behind the study at all – only the wall of the corridor, as far as he could see. It was more and more mysterious.

He went back to the study again, and over to the bookcase. Yes – there it was again. *Somebody* was asleep and snoring not far off – but WHERE?

Julian began to examine the bookcase. It was full of books jammed tightly together – novels, biographies, reference books – all higgledy-piggledy. He removed some from a shelf and examined the bookcase behind. It was of solid wood.

He put back the books and examined the big bookcase again. It was a very solid affair. Julian looked carefully at the books, shining in the moonlight. One shelf of books looked different from the others – less tidy – the books not so jammed together. Why should just one shelf be different?

Julian quietly took the books from that shelf. Behind them was the solid wood again. Julian put his hand at the back and felt about. A knob was hidden in a corner. A knob! Whatever was that there for?

Cautiously Julian turned the knob this way and that. Nothing happened. Then he pressed it. Still nothing happened. He pulled it – and it slid out a good six inches!

Then the whole of the back of that particular shelf slid quietly downwards, and left an opening big enough for somebody to squeeze through! Julian held his breath. A sliding panel! What was behind it?

A dim flickering light came from the space behind.

Julian waited till his eyes were used to it after the bright moonlight. He was trembling with excitement. The snoring now sounded so loud that Julian felt as if the snorer must be almost within hand's reach!

Then gradually he made out a tiny room, with a small narrow bed, a table and a shelf on which a few articles could dimly be made out. A candle was burning in a corner. On the bed was the snorer. Julian could not see what he was like, except that he looked big and burly as he lay there, snoring peacefully.

'What a find!' thought Julian. 'A secret hiding-place – a place to hide all kinds of people, I suppose, who have

enough money to pay for such a safe hole. This fellow ought to have been warned not to snore! He gave himself away.'

The body did not dare to stay there any longer, looking into that curious secret room. It must be built in a space between the wall of the study and the wall of the corridor – probably a very old hiding-place made when the house was built.

Julian felt for the knob. He pushed it back into place, and the panel slid up again, as noiselessly as before. It was evidently kept in good working order!

The snoring was muffled again now. Julian replaced the books, hoping that they were more or less as he had found them.

He felt very thrilled. He had found one of the secrets of Owl's Dene, at any rate. The police would be *very* interested to hear about that secret hole – and perhaps they would be even more interested to hear about the person inside it!

It was absolutely essential now that he and the others should escape. Would it be all right if he went without Dick? No – if the men suspected any dirty work on his part – discovered that he knew of the secret hole, for instance – they might harm Dick. Regretfully Julian decided that there must be no escape for him unless everyone, including Dick, could come too.

He didn't explore any more. He suddenly felt very tired indeed and crept softly upstairs. He felt as if he simply must lie down and think. He was too tired to do anything else.

He went to the bedroom. The key was still in the lock outside. He went into the room and shut the door. Mr Perton would find the door unlocked the next morning, but probably he would think he hadn't turned the key properly. Julian lay down on the mattress beside Richard. All the others were fast asleep.

He meant to think out all his problems – but no sooner had he closed his eyes than he was fast asleep. He didn't hear Timmy howling outside once more. He didn't hear the screech owl that made the night hideous on the hill. He didn't see the moon slide down the sky.

It was not Mr Perton who awoke the children next morning, but the woman. She came into the room and called to them.

'If you want breakfast you'd better come down and have it!'

They all sat up in a hurry, wondering where in the world they were. 'Hallo!' said Julian, blinking sleepily. 'Breakfast, did you say? It sounds good. Is there anywhere we can wash?'

'You can wash down in the kitchen,' said the woman, sullenly, 'I'm not cleaning any bathroom up after you!'

'Leave the door unlocked for us to get out!' said Julian, innocently. 'Mr Perton locked it last night.'

'So he said,' answered the woman, 'but he *hadn't* locked it! It wasn't locked when I tried the door this morning. Aha! You didn't know that, did you? You'd have been wandering all over the house, I suppose, if you'd guessed that.'

'Probably we should,' agreed Julian, winking at the others. They knew that he had meant to go and find Dick in the night, and snoop round a bit – but they didn't know all he had discovered. He hadn't had the heart to wake them and tell them the night before.

'Don't you be too long,' said the woman, and went out of the door, leaving it open.

'I hope she's taken some breakfast up to poor old Dick,' said Julian, in a low voice. The others came close to him.

'Ju – did you find Dick last night?' whispered Anne. He nodded. Then, very quickly and quietly he told them all he had discovered – where Dick was – and then how he had heard the snoring – and discovered the secret panel – the hidden room – and the man who slept so soundly there, not knowing that Julian had seen him.

'Julian! How thrilling!' said George. 'Whoever would have thought of all that?'

'Oh yes – and I discovered the machinery that opens the gates too,' said Julian. 'It's in the same room. But come on – if we don't go down to the kitchen that woman will be after us again. I hope Hunchy won't be there – I don't like him.'

Hunchy, however, *was* there, finishing his breakfast at a small table. He scowled at the children, but they took absolutely no notice of him.

'You've been a long time,' grumbled the woman. 'There's the sink over there, if you want to wash, and I've put a towel out for you. You look pretty dirty, all of you.'

'We are,' said Julian, cheerfully. 'We could have done with a bath last night – but we didn't exactly get much of a welcome, you know.'

When they had washed they went to a big scrubbed table. There was no cloth on it. The woman had put out some bread and butter and some boiled eggs and a jug of steaming hot cocoa. They all sat down and began to help themselves. Julian talked cheerfully, winking at the others to make them do the same. He wasn't going to let the hunchback think they were scared or worried in any way.

'Shut up, you,' said Hunchy, suddenly. Julian took no notice. He went on talking, and George backed him up valiantly, though Anne and Richard were too scared, after hearing the hunchback's furious voice.

'Did you hear what I said?' suddenly yelled Hunchy, and got up from the little table where he had been sitting. 'Hold your tongues, all of you! Coming into my kitchen and making all that row! Hold your tongues!'

Julian rose too. 'I don't take orders from you whoever you are,' he said, and he sounded just like a grown-up. 'You hold your tongue – or else be civil.'

'Oh, don't talk to him like that, don't,' begged the woman, anxiously. 'He's got such a temper – he'll take a stick to you!'

'I'd take a stick to *him* – except that I don't hit fellows smaller than myself,' said Julian.

What would have happened if Mr Perton hadn't appeared in the kitchen at that moment nobody knew! He stalked in and glared round, sensing that there was a row going on.

'You losing your temper again, Hunchy?' he said. 'Keep it till it's needed. I'll ask you to produce it sometime today possibly – if these kids don't behave themselves!' He looked round at the children with a grim expression. Then he glanced at the woman.

'Rooky's coming soon,' he told her. 'And one or two others. Get a meal – a good one. Keep these children in here, Hunchy, and keep an eye on them. I may want them later.'

He went out. The woman was trembling. 'Rooky's coming,' she half-whispered to Hunchy.

'Get on with your work, woman,' said the dwarf. 'Go out and get the vegetables in yourself – I've got to keep an eye on these kids.'

The poor woman scuttled about. Anne was sorry for her. She went over to her. 'Shall I clear away and wash up for you?' she asked. 'You're going to be busy – and I've nothing to do.'

'We'll all help,' said Julian. The woman gave him an astonished and grateful glance. It was plain that she was not used to good manners or politeness of any sort.

'Yah!' said Hunchy, sneeringly. 'You won't get round *me* with your smarmy ways!'

Nobody took the slightest notice of him. All the children began to clear away the breakfast things, and Anne and George stacked them in the sink, and began to wash them.

'Yah!' said Hunchy again.

'And yah to you,' said Julian, pleasantly, which made the others laugh, and Hunchy scowl till his eyes disappeared under his brows!

14

Rooky is very angry

About an hour later there was a curious grinding, groaning noise that turned to a whining. Richard, Anne and George jumped violently. But Julian knew what it was.

'The gates are being opened,' he told them, and they remembered how he had described the machinery that opened the gates – the curious wheel-like handle, labelled 'Left Gate. Right Gate. Both Gates'.

'How do *you* know that?' asked Hunchy at once, surprised and suspicious.

'Oh, I'm a good guesser,' replied Julian airily. 'Correct me if I'm wrong – but I couldn't help thinking the gates were being opened – and I'm guessing it's Rooky that's coming through them!'

'You're so sharp you'll cut yourself one day,' grumbled Hunchy, going to the door.

'So my mother told me when I was two years old,' said Julian, and the others giggled. If there was any answering back to be done, Julian could always do it!

They all went to the window. George opened it. Timmy

was there, sitting just outside. George had begged the woman to let him in, but she wouldn't. She had thrown him some scraps, and told George there was a pond he could drink from, but beyond that she wouldn't go.

'Timmy,' called George, as she heard the sound of a car purring quietly up the drive, 'Timmy – stay there. Don't move!'

She was afraid that Timmy might perhaps run round to the front door, and go for anyone who jumped out of the car. Timmy looked up at her inquiringly. He was puzzled about this whole affair. Why wasn't he allowed inside the house with George? He knew there were some people who didn't welcome dogs into their houses – but George never went to those houses. It was a puzzle to him, too, to understand why she didn't come out to him.

Still, she was there, leaning out of the window; he could hear her voice; he could even lick her hand if he stood up on his hind legs against the wall.

'You shut that window and come inside,' said Hunchy, maliciously. He took quite a pleasure in seeing that George was upset at being separated from Timmy.

'Here comes the car,' said Julian. They all looked at it – and then glanced at each other. KMF 102 – of course!

The black Bentley swept by the kitchen windows and up to the front door. Three men got out. Richard crouched back, his face going pale.

Julian glanced round at him raising his eyebrows, mutely asking him if he recognized one of the men as Rooky. Richard nodded miserably. He was very frightened now.

The whining, groaning noise came again. The gates were being shut. Voices came from the hall, then the men went into one of the rooms, and there was the sound of a door being shut.

Julian wondered if he could slip out of the room unnoticed and go up to see if Dick was all right. He sidled to the door, thinking that Hunchy was engrossed in cleaning an array of dirty shoes. But his grating voice sounded at once.

'Where you going? If you don't obey orders I'll tell Mr Perton – and won't you be sorry!'

'There's quite a lot of people in his house going to be sorry for themselves soon,' said Julian, in an irritatingly cheerful voice. 'You be careful, Hunchy.'

Hunchy lost his temper suddenly and threw the shoe-brush he was using straight at Julian. Julian caught it deftly and threw it up on the high mantelpiece.

'Thanks,' he said. 'Like to throw another?'

'Oh don't,' said the woman, beseechingly. 'You don't know what he's like when he's in a real temper. Don't!'

The door of the room that the men had gone into opened, and somebody went upstairs. 'To fetch Dick,' thought Julian at once. He stood and listened.

Hunchy got another shoe-brush and went on polishing, muttering angrily under his breath. The woman went on preparing some food. The others listened with Julian. They too guessed that the man had gone to fetch Dick to show him to Rooky.

Footsteps came down the stairs again – two lots this time. Yes – Dick must be with the man, they could hear his voice.

'Let go my arm! I can come without being dragged!' they heard him say indignantly. Good old Dick! He wasn't going to be dragged about without making a strong protest.

He was taken into the room where the other three men were waiting. Then a loud voice was heard.

'He's not the boy! Fools – you've got the wrong boy!'

Hunchy and the woman heard the words too. They gaped at one another. Something had gone wrong. They went to the door and stood there silently. The children just stood behind them. Julian edged Richard away very gradually.

'Rub some soot over your hair,' he whispered. 'Make it as black as you can, Richard. If the men come out here to see us, they're not likely to recognize you so easily if your hair's black. Go on, quick – while the others aren't paying attention.'

Julian was pointing to the inside of the grate, where black soot hung. Richard put his trembling hands into it and covered with it. Then he rubbed the soot over his yellow hair.

'More,' whispered Julian. 'Much more! Go on. I'll stand in front of you so that the others can't see what you're doing.'

Richard rubbed soot even more wildly over his hair. Julian nodded. Yes – it looked black enough now. Richard looked quite different. Julian hoped Anne and George would be sensible enough not to exclaim when they saw him.

There was evidently some sharp argument going on in the room off the hall. Voices were raised, but not many words could be made out from where the children stood at the kitchen door. Dick's voice could be heard too. It suddenly sounded quite clearly.

'I TOLD you you'd made a mistake. Now you just let me go, see!'

Hunchy suddenly pushed everyone roughly away from the door – except poor Richard who was standing over in a dark corner, shaking with fright!

'They're coming,' he hissed. 'Get away from the door.'

Everyone obeyed. Hunchy took up a shoe-brush again, the woman went to peel potatoes, the children turned over the pages of some old magazines they had found.

Footsteps came to the kitchen door. It was flung open. Mr Perton was there – and behind him another man. No mistaking who *he* was!

Thick-lipped, with an enormous nose – yes, he was the ruffian Rooky, once bodyguard to Richard's father – the man who hated Richard because he had told tales of him and who had been sent off in disgrace by the boy's father.

Richard cowered back in his corner, hiding behind the others. Anne and George had given him astonished stares when they had noticed his hair, but neither of them had said a word. Hunchy and the woman didn't seem to have noticed any change in him.

Dick was with the two men. He waved to the others. Julian grinned. Good old Dick!

Rooky glanced at all four children. His eye rested for a moment on Richard, and then glanced away. He hadn't recognized him!

'Well, Mr Perton,' said Julian. 'I'm glad to see you've got my brother down from the room you locked him up in last night. I imagine that means he can come with us now. Why you brought him here as you did, and made him a prisoner last night I can't imagine.'

'Now look here,' said Mr Perton, in quite a different voice from the one he had used to them before, 'now look here – quite frankly we made a mistake. You don't need to know why or how – that's none of your business. This isn't the boy we wanted.'

'We *told* you he was our brother,' said Anne.

'Quite,' said Mr Perton, politely. 'I am sorry I disbelieved you. These things happen. Now – we want to make you all a handsome present for any inconvenience you have suffered – er – ten pounds for you to spend on ice-creams and so on. You can go whenever you like.'

'And don't try and tell any fairy stories to anyone,' said Rooky suddenly, in a threatening voice. 'See? We made a mistake – but we're not having it talked about. If you say anything silly, we shall say that we found this boy lost in the woods, took pity on him and brought him here for the night – and that you kids were – found trespassing in the grounds. You understand?'

'I understand perfectly,' said Julian, in a cool rather scornful voice. 'Well – I take it we can all go now, then?'

'Yes,' said Mr Perton. He put his hand into his pocket and took out some pound notes. He handed two to each of the children. They glanced at Julian to see if they were to take them or not. Not one of them felt willing to accept Mr Perton's money. But they knew they must take them if Julian did.

Julian accepted the two notes handed to him, and pocketed them without a word of thanks. The others did the same. Richard kept his head down well all the time, hoping that the two men would not notice how his knees were shaking. He was really terrified of Rooky.

'Now clear out,' said Rooky when the ten pounds had been divided. 'Forget all this – or you'll be very sorry.'

He opened the door that led into the garden. The children trooped out silently, Richard well in their midst. Timmy was waiting for them. He gave a loud bark of welcome and flung himself on George, fawning on her, licking every bit of her he could reach. He looked back at the kitchen door and gave a questioning growl as if to say, 'Do you want me to go for anyone in there?'

'No,' said George. 'You come with us, Timmy. We'll get out of here as quickly as we can.'

'Give me your pound notes, quick,' said Julian in a low voice, when they had rounded a corner and were out of sight of the windows. They all handed them to him wonderingly. What was he going to do with them?

The woman had come out to watch them go. Julian beckoned to her. She came hesitatingly down the garden. 'For you,' said Julian, putting the notes into her hand. 'We don't want them.'

The woman took them, amazed. Her eyes filled with

tears. 'Why – it's a fortune – no, no, you take them back. You're kind, though – so kind.'

Julian turned away, leaving the astonished and delighted woman standing staring after them. He hurried after the others.

'That was a very, very good idea of yours,' said Anne, warmly, and the others agreed. All of them had been sorry for the poor woman.

'Come on,' said Julian. 'We don't want to miss the opening of the gates! Listen – can you hear the groaning noise back at the house. Somebody has set the machinery working that opens the gates. Thank goodness we're free – and Richard too. That *was* a bit of luck!'

'Yes, I was so scared Rooky would recognize me, even though my hair was sooted black,' said Richard, who was now looking much more cheerful. 'Oh look – we can see the end of the drive now – and the gates are wide open. We're free!'

'We'll get our bikes,' said Julian. 'I know where we left them. You can ride on my crossbar Richard, because we're a bike short. Dick must have his bike back now – you remember you borrowed it? Look – here they are.'

They mounted their bicycles and began to cycle down the drive – and then Anne gave a scream.

'Julian! Look, look – the gates are closing again. Quick, quick – we'll be left inside!'

Everyone saw in horror that the gates were actually closing, very slowly. They pedalled as fast as they could – but it was no use. By the time they got there the two great gates were fast shut. No amount of shaking would open them. And just as they were so very nearly out!

15

Prisoners

They all flung themselves down on the grass verge and groaned.

'What have they done that for, just as we were going out?' said Dick. 'Was it a mistake, do you think? I mean – did they think we'd had time to go out, or what?'

'Well – if it was a mistake, it's easy to put right,' said Julian. 'I'll just cycle back to the house and tell them they shut the gates too soon.'

'Yes – you do that,' said George. 'We'll wait here.'

But before Julian could even mount his bicycle there came the sound of the car purring down the long drive. All the children jumped to their feet. Richard ran behind a bush in panic. He was terrified of having to face Rooky again.

The car drew up by the children and stopped. 'Yes, they're still here,' said Mr Perton's voice, as he got out of the car. Rooky got out too. They came over to the children.

Rooky ran his eyes over them. 'Where's that other boy?' he asked quickly.

'I can't imagine,' said Julian, coolly. 'Dear me – I wonder if he had time to cycle out of the gateway. Why did you shut the gates so soon, Mr Perton?'

Rooky had caught sight of Richard's shivering figure behind the bush. He strode over to him and yanked him out. He looked at him closely. Then he pulled him over to Mr Perton.

'Yes – I thought so – *this* is the boy we want! He's sooted his hair or something, and that's why I didn't recognize him. But when he'd gone I felt sure there was something familiar about him – that's why I wanted another look.' He shook poor Richard like a dog shaking a rat.

'Well – what do you want to do about it?' asked Mr Perton, rather gloomily.

'Hold him, of course,' said Rooky. 'I'll get back at his father now – he'll have to pay a very large sum of money for his horrible son! That'll be useful, won't it? And I can pay this kid out for some of the lies he told his father about me. Nasty little rat.'

He shook Richard again. Julian stepped forward, white and furious.

'Now you stop that,' he said. 'Let the boy go. Haven't you done enough already – keeping my brother locked up for nothing – holding us all for the night – and now you talk about kidnapping! Haven't you just come out of prison? Do you want to go back there?'

Rooky dropped Richard and lunged out at Julian. With a snarl Timmy flung himself between them and bit the man's hand. Rooky let out a howl of rage and nursed his injured hand. He yelled at Julian.

'Call that dog to heel. Do you hear?'

'I'll call him to heel all right – if you talk sense,' said Julian, still white with rage. 'You're going to let us all go, here and now. Go back and open these gates.'

Timmy growled terrifyingly, and both Rooky and Mr

Perton took some hurried steps backwards. Rooky picked up a very big stone.

'If you dare to throw that I'll set my dog on you again!' shouted George, in sudden fear. Mr Perton knocked the stone out of Rooky's hand.

'Don't be a fool,' he said. 'That dog could make mince-meat of us – great ugly brute. Look at his teeth. For goodness' sake let the kids go, Rooky.'

'Not till we've finished our plans,' said Rooky fiercely, still nursing his hand. 'Keep 'em all prisoners here! We shan't be long before our jobs are done. And what's more

I'm going to take that little rat there off with me when I go! Ha! I'll teach him a few things – and his father too.'

Timmy growled again. He was straining at George's hand. She had him firmly by the collar. Richard trembled when he heard Rooky's threats about him. Tears ran down his face.

'Yes – you can howl all you like,' said Rooky, scowling at him. 'You wait till I get you! Miserable little coward – you never did have any spunk – you just ran round telling tales and misbehaving yourself whenever you could.'

'Look, Rooky – you'd better come up to the house and have that hand seen to,' said Mr Perton. 'It's bleeding badly. You ought to wash it and put some stuff on it – you know a dog's bite is dangerous. Come on. You can deal with these kids afterwards.'

Rooky allowed himself to be led back to the car. He shook his unhurt fist at the children as they watched silently.

'Interfering brats! Little . . .'

But the rest of his pleasant words were lost in the purring of the car's engine. Mr Perton backed a little, turned the car, and it disappeared up the drive. The five children sat themselves down on the grass verge. Richard began to sob out loud.

'Do shut up, Richard,' said George. 'Rooky was right when he said you were a little coward, with no spunk. So you are. Anne's much pluckier than you are. I wish to goodness we had never met you.'

Richard rubbed his hands over his eyes. They were sooty, and made his face look most peculiar with streaks of black soot mixed with his tears. He tooked very woe-begone indeed.

'I'm sorry,' he sniffed. 'I know you don't believe me – but I really am. I've always been a bit of a coward – I can't help it.'

'Yes you can,' said Julian, scornfully. 'Anybody can

help being a coward. Cowardice is just thinking of your own miserable skin instead of somebody else's. Why, even little Anne is more worried about *us* than she is about herself – and that makes her brave. She couldn't be a coward if she tried.'

This was a completely new idea to Richard. He tried to wipe his face dry. 'I'll try to be like you,' he said, in a muffled voice. 'You're all so decent. I've never had friends like you before. Honestly, I won't let you down again.'

'Well, we'll see,' said Julian, doubtfully. 'It would certainly be a surprise if you turned into a hero all of a sudden – a very *nice* surprise, of course – but in the meantime it would be a help if you stopped howling for a bit and let us talk.'

Richard subsided. He really looked very peculiar with his soot-streaked face. Julian turned to the others.

'This is maddening!' he said. 'Just as we so nearly got out. I suppose they'll shut us up in some room and keep us there till they've finished whatever this "job" is. I imagine the "job" consists of getting that hidden fellow away in safety – the one I saw in the secret room.'

'Won't Richard's people report his disappearance to the police?' said George, fondling Timmy, who wouldn't stop licking her now he had got her again.

'Yes, they will. But what good will that do? The police won't have the faintest notion where he is,' said Julian. 'Nobody knows where we are, either, come to that – but Aunt Fanny won't worry yet, because she knows we're off on a cycling tour, and wouldn't be writing to her anyway.'

'Do you think those men will really take me off with them when they go?' asked Richard.

'Well, we'll hope we shall have managed to escape before that,' said Julian, not liking to say yes, certainly Richard would be whisked away!

'How *can* we escape?' asked Anne. 'We'd never get over those high walls. And I don't expect anyone ever comes by here – right at the top of this deserted hill. No tradesman would ever call.'

'What about the postman?' asked Anne.

'They probably arrange to fetch their post each day,' said Julian. 'I don't expect they want anyone coming here at all. Or – there may be a letter-box outside the gate. I never thought of that!'

They went to see. But although they craned their necks to see each side, there didn't seem to be any letter-box at all for the postman to slip letters in. So the faint hope that had risen in their minds, that they might catch the postman and give him a message, vanished at once.

'Hallo – here's the woman – Aggie, or whatever he name is,' said George, suddenly, as Timmy growled. They all turned their heads. Yes, Aggie was coming down the drive in a hurry – could she be going out? Would the gates open for her?

Their hopes died as she came near. 'Oh, there you are! I've come with a message. You can do one of two things – you can stay out in the grounds all day, and not put foot into the house at all – or you can come into the house and be locked up in one of the rooms.'

She looked round cautiously and lowered her voice. 'I'm sorry you didn't get out; right down upset I am. It's bad enough for an old woman like me, being cooped up here with Hunchy – but it's not right to keep children in this place. You're nice children too.'

'Thanks,' said Julian. 'Now, seeing that you think we're so nice – tell us, is there any way we can get out besides going through these gates?'

'No. No way at all,' said the woman. 'It's like a prison, once those gates are shut. Nobody's allowed in, and you're only allowed out if it suits Mr Perton and the others. So don't try to escape – it's hopeless.'

Nobody said anything to that. Aggie glanced over her shoulder as if she feared somebody might be listening –

Hunchy perhaps – and went on in a low voice.

'Mr Perton said I wasn't to give you much food. And he said Hunchy's to put down food for the dog with poison in it – so don't you let him eat any but what I give you myself.'

'The brute,' cried George, and she held Timmy close against her. 'Did you hear that, Timmy? It's a pity you didn't bite Mr Perton too!'

'Sh!' said the woman, afraid. 'I didn't ought to tell you all this, you know that – but you're kind, and you gave me all that money. Right down nice you are. Now you listen to me – you'd better say you'd rather keep out here in the grounds – because if you're locked up I wouldn't dare to bring you much food in case Rooky came in and saw it. But if you stay out here it's easier. I can give you plenty.'

'Thank you very much,' said Julian, and the others nodded too. 'In any case we'd rather be out here. I suppose Mr Perton is afraid we'd stumble on some of his queer secrets in the house if we had the free run there! All right – tell him we'll be in the grounds. What about our food? How shall we manage about that? We don't want to get you into trouble – but we're very hungry for our meals, and we really could do with a good dinner today.'

'I'll manage it for you,' said Aggie, and she actually smiled. 'But mind what I say now – don't you let that dog eat anything Hunchy puts down for him! It'll be poisoned.'

A voice shouted from the house. Aggie jerked her head up and listened. 'That's Hunchy,' she said. 'I must go.'

She hurried back up the drive. 'Well, well, well,' said Julian, 'so they thought they'd poison old Timmy, did they? They'll have to think again, old fellow, won't they?'

'Woof,' said Timmy, gravely, and didn't even wag his tail!

16

Aggie – and Hunchy

'I feel as if I want some exercise,' said George, when Aggie had gone. 'Let's explore the grounds. You never know what we might find!'

They got up, glad of something to do to take their minds off their surprising problems. Really, who would have thought yesterday, when they were happily cycling along sunny country roads, that they would be held prisoner like this today? You just never knew what would happen. It made life exciting, of course – but it did spoil a cycling tour!

They found absolutely nothing of interest in the grounds except a couple of cows, a large number of hens, and a brood of young ducklings. Evidently even the milkman didn't need to call at Owl's Dene! It was quite self-contained.

'I expect that black Bentley goes down each day to some town or other, to collect letters, and to buy meat, or fish,' said George. 'Otherwise Owl's Dene could keep itself going for months on end if necessary without any contact with the outside world. I expect they've got stacks and stacks of tinned food.'

'It's weird to find a place like this, tucked away on a deserted hill, forgotten by everyone – guarding goodness knows what secrets,' said Dick. 'I'd love to know who that man was you saw in the secret room, Julian – the snorer!'

'Someone who doesn't want to be seen even by Hunchy or Aggie,' said Julian. 'Someone the police would dearly love to see, I expect!'

'I *wish* we could get out of here,' said George, longingly. 'I hate the place. It's got such a nasty "feel" about it. And I hate the thought of somebody trying to poison Timmy.'

'Don't worry – he won't be poisoned,' said Dick. 'We won't let him be. He can have half *our* food, can't you, Timmy, old fellow?'

Timmy agreed. He woofed and wagged his tail. He wouldn't leave George's side that morning, but stuck to her like a leech.

'Well, we've been all round the grounds and there's nothing much to see,' said Julian, when they had come back near the house. 'I suppose Hunchy sees to the milking and feeds the poultry and brings in the vegetables. Aggie has to manage the house. I say – look – there's Hunchy now. He's putting down food for Timmy!

Hunchy was making signs to them. 'Here's the dog's dinner!' he yelled.

'Don't say a word, George,' said Julian in a low voice. 'We'll pretend to let Timmy eat it, but we'll really throw it away somewhere – and he'll be frightfully astonished when Timmy is still all-alive-o tomorrow morning!'

Hunchy disappeared in the direction of the cow-shed, carrying a pail. Anne gave a little giggle.

'I know what we'll pretend! We'll pretend that Timmy ate half and didn't like the rest – so we gave it to the hens and ducks!'

'And Hunchy will be frightfully upset because he'll

think they'll die and he'll get into a row,' said George.
'Serve him right! Come on – let's get the food now.'

She ran to pick up the big bowl of food. Timmy sniffed
at it and turned away. It was obvious that he wouldn't
have fancied it much even if George had allowed him to
have it. Timmy was a very sensible dog.

'Quick, get that spade, Ju, and dig a hole before
Hunchy comes back,' said George, and Julian set to work
grinning. It didn't take him more than a minute to dig a
large hole in the soft earth of a bed. George emptied all the
food into the hole, wiped the bowl round with a handful of
leaves and watched Julian filling in the earth. Now no
animals could get at the poisoned food.

'Let's go to the hen-run now, and when we see Hunchy
we'll wave to him,' said Julian. 'He'll ask us what we've
been doing. Come on. He deserves to have a shock.'

They went to the hen-house, and stood looking through the wire surrounding the hen-run. As Hunchy came along they turned and waved to him. George pretended to scrape some scraps out of the dog's bowl into the run. Hunchy stared hard. Then he ran towards her, shouting.

'Don't do that, don't do that!'

'What's the matter?' asked George, innocently, pretending to push some scraps through the wire. 'Can't I give the hens some scraps?'

'Is that the bowl I put the dog's food down in?' asked Hunchy, sharply.

'Yes,' said George.

'And he didn't eat all the food – so you're giving it to my hens!' shouted Hunchy in a rage, and snatched the bowl out of George's hands. She pretended to be very angry.

'Don't! Why shouldn't your hens have scraps from the dog's bowl? The food you gave Timmy looked very nice – can't the hens have some?'

Hunchy looked into the hen-run with a groan. The hens were pecking about near the children for all the world as if they were eating something just thrown to them. Hunchy felt sure they would all be dead by the next day – and then, what trouble he would get into!

He glared at George. 'Idiot of a boy! Giving my hens that food! You deserve a good whipping.'

He thought George was a boy, of course. The others looked on with interest. It served Hunchy right to get into a panic over his hens, after trying to poison dear old Timmy.

Hunchy didn't seem to know what to do. Eventually he took a stiff brush from a nearby shed and went into the hen-run. He had evidently decided to sweep the whole place in case any poisoned bits of food were still left about. He swept laboriously and the children watched him, pleased that he should punish himself in this way.

'I've never seen anyone bother to sweep a hen-run

before,' said Dick, in a loud and interested voice.

'Nor have I,' said George at once. 'He must be very anxious to bring his hens up properly.'

'It's jolly hard work, I should think,' said Julian. 'Glad I haven't got to do it. Pity to sweep up all the bits of food, though. An awful waste.'

Everyone agreed heartily to this.

'Funny he should be so upset about my giving the hens any scraps of the food he put down for Timmy,' said George. 'I mean – it seems a bit *suspicious*.'

'It does rather,' agreed Dick. 'But then perhaps he's a suspicious character.'

Hunchy could hear all this quite plainly. The children meant him to, of course. He stopped his sweeping and scowled evilly at them.

'Clear off, you little pests,' he said, and raised his broom as if to rush at the children with it.

'He looks like an angry hen,' said Anne, joining in.

'He's just going to cluck,' put in Richard, and the others laughed. Hunchy ran to open the gate of the hen-run, red with anger.

'Of course – it's just struck me – he *might* have put poison into Timmy's bowl of food,' said Julian, loudly. 'That's why he's so upset about his hens. Dear, dear – how true the old proverb is – he that digs a pit shall fall into it himself!'

The mention of poison stopped Hunchy's rush at once. He flung the broom into the shed, and made off for the house without another word.

'Well – we gave him a bit more than he bargained for,' said Julian.

'And you needn't worry, hens,' said Anne, putting her face to the wire-netting of the run. 'You're not poisoned – and we wouldn't *dream* of harming you!'

'Aggie's calling us,' said Richard. 'Look – perhaps she's got some food for us.'

'I hope so,' said Dick. 'I'm getting very hungry. It's funny that grown-ups never seem to get as hungry as children. I do pity them.'

'Why? Do you *like* being hungry?' said Anne as they walked over to the house.

'Yes, if I know there's a good meal in the offing,' said Dick. 'Otherwise it wouldn't be at all funny. Oh goodness – is this all that Aggie has provided?'

On the window-sill was a loaf of stale-looking bread and a piece of very hard yellow cheese. Nothing else at all. Hunchy was there, grinning.

'Aggie says that's your dinner,' he said, and sat himself down at the table to spoon out enormous helpings of a very savoury stew.

'A little revenge for our behaviour by the hen-run,' murmured Julian softly. 'Well, well – I thought better than this of Aggie. I wonder where she is.'

She came out of the kitchen door at that moment, carrying a washing-basket that appeared to be full of clothes. 'I'll just hang these out, Hunchy, and I'll be back,' she called to him. She turned to the children and gave them a broad wink.

'There's your dinner on the window-sill,' she said. 'Get it and take it somewhere to eat. Hunchy and me don't want you round the kitchen.'

She suddenly smiled and nodded her head down towards the washing-basket. The children understood immediately. Their real dinner was in there!

They snatched the bread and cheese from the sill and followed her. She set down the basket under a tree, where it was well-hidden from the house. A clothes-line stretched there. 'I'll be out afterwards to hang my washing,' she said, and with another smile that changed her whole face, she went back to the house.

'Good old Aggie,' said Julian, lifting up the top cloth in the basket. 'My word – just look here!'

17

Julian has a bright idea

Aggie had managed to pack knives, forks, spoons, plates and mugs into the bottom of the basket. There were two big bottles of milk. There was a large meat-pie with delicious looking pastry on top, and a collection of buns, biscuits and oranges. There were also some home-made sweets. Aggie had certainly been very generous!

All the things were quickly whipped out of the basket. The children carried them behind the bushes, sat down and proceeded to eat a first-rate dinner. Timmy got his share of the meat-pie and biscuits. He also gobbled up a large part of the hard yellow cheese.

'Now we'd better rinse everything under that garden tap over there, and then pack them neatly into the bottom of the basket again,' said Julian. 'We don't want to get Aggie into any sort of trouble for her kindness.'

The dishes were soon rinsed and packed back into the basket. The clothes were drawn over them – nothing could be seen!

Aggie came outside to them in about half an hour. The children went to her and spoke in low voices.

'Thanks, Aggie, that was super!'

'You *are* a brick. We did enjoy it!'

'I bet Hunchy didn't enjoy his dinner as much as *we* did!'

'Sh!' said Aggie, half-pleased and half-scared. 'You never know when Hunchy's listening. He's got ears like a hare! Listen – I'll be coming out to get the eggs from the hen-run at tea-time. I'll have a basket with me for the eggs – and I shall have your tea in it. I'll leave your tea in the hen-house when I get the eggs. You can fetch it when I've gone.'

'You're a wonder, Aggie!' said Julian, admiringly. 'You really are.'

Aggie looked pleased. It was plain that nobody had said a kind or admiring word to her for years and years. She was a poor, miserable, scared old woman – but she was quite enjoying this little secret. She was pleased at getting the better of Hunchy too. Perhaps she felt it was some slight revenge for all the years he had ill-treated her.

She hung out some of the clothes in the basket, left one in to cover the dinner-things, and then went back into the house.

'Poor old thing,' said Dick. 'What a life!'

'Yes – *I* shouldn't like to be cooped up here for years and years with ruffians like Perton and Rooky,' said Julian.

'It looks as if we shall be if we don't hurry up and think of some plan of escape,' said Dick.

'Yes. We'd better think hard again,' said Julian. 'Come over to those trees there. We can sit on the grass under them and talk without being overheard anywhere.'

'Look – Hunchy is polishing the black Bentley,' said George. 'I'll just pass near him with Timmy, and let Timmy growl. He'll see Timmy's all alive and kicking then.'

So she took Timmy near the Bentley, and of course he

growled horribly when he came upon Hunchy. Hunchy promptly got into the car and shut the door. George grinned.

'Hallo!' she said. 'Going off for a ride? Can Timmy and I come with you?'

She made as if she was going to open the door, and Hunchy yelled loudly: 'Don't you let that dog in here! I've seen Rooky's hand – one finger's very bad indeed. I don't want that dog going for *me*.'

'Do take me for a ride with you, Hunchy,' persisted George. 'Timmy loves cars.'

'Go away,' said Hunchy, hanging on to the door-handle for dear life. 'I've got to get this car cleaned up for Mr Perton this evening. You let me get out and finish the job.'

George laughed and went off to join the others. 'Well, he can see Timmy's all-alive-o,' said Dick, with a grin. 'Good thing too. We'd find ourselves in a much bigger fix if we hadn't got old Timmy to protect us.'

They went over to the clump of trees and sat down. 'What was it that Hunchy said about the car?' asked Julian. George told him. Julian looked thoughtful. Anne knew that look – it meant that Julian was thinking of a plan! She prodded him.

'Ju! You've got a plan, haven't you? What is it?'

'Well – I'm only just wondering about something,' said Julian, slowly. 'That car – and the fact that Mr Perton is going out in it tonight – which means he will go out through those gates . . .'

'What of it?' said Dick. 'Thinking of going with him?'

'Well, yes, I was,' said Julian, surprisingly. 'You see – if he's not going till dark, I think I could probably get into the boot – and hide there till the car stops somewhere, and then I could open the boot, get out, and go off for help!'

Everyone looked at him in silence. Anne's eyes gleamed. 'Oh Julian! It's a wizard plan.'

'It sounds jolly good,' said Dick.

'The only thing is – I don't like being left here without Julian,' said Anne, suddenly feeling scared. 'Everything's all right if Julian's here.'

'*I* could go,' said Dick.

'Or I could,' said George, 'only there wouldn't be room for Timmy too.'

'The boot looks pretty big from outside,' said Julian. 'I wish I could take Anne with me. Then I'd know she was safe. You others would be all right so long as you had Timmy.'

They discussed the matter thoroughly. They dropped it towards tea-time when they saw Aggie coming out with a basket to collect the eggs. She made a sign to them not to come over to her. Possibly someone was watching. They stayed where they were, and watched her go into the hen-house. She remained there a short time, and then came out with a basketful of new-laid eggs. She walked to the house without looking at the children again.

'I'll go and see if she's left anything in the hen-house,' said Dick, and went over to it. He soon appeared again, grinning. His pockets bulged!

Aggie had left about two dozen potted-meat sandwiches, a big slab of cherry cake and a bottle of milk. The children went under the bushes and Dick unloaded his pockets. 'She even left a bone for old Tim,' he said.

'I suppose it's all right,' said George doubtfully. Julian smelt it.

'Perfectly fresh,' he said. 'No poison here at all! Anyway, Aggie wouldn't play a dirty trick like that. Come on – let's tuck in.'

They were very bored after tea, so Julian arranged some races and some jumping competitions. Timmy, of course, would have won them all if he had been counted as a proper competitor. But he wasn't. He went in for everything, though, and barked so excitedly that Mr Perton came to a window and yelled to him to stop.

'Sorry!' yelled back George. 'Timmy's so full of beans today, you see!'

'Mr Perton will be wondering why,' said Julian, with a grin. 'He'll be rowing Hunchy for not getting on with the poison job.'

When it began to grow dark the children went cautiously to the car. Hunchy had finished working on it. Quietly Julian opened the boot and looked inside. He gave an exclamation of disappointment.

'It's only a small one! I can't get in there, I'm afraid. Nor can you, Dick.'

'I'll go then,' said Anne, in a small voice.

'Certainly not,' said Julian.

'Well – *I'll* go,' said Richard, surprisingly. 'I could just about squash in there.'

'*You!*' said Dick. 'You'd be scared stiff.'

Richard was silent for a moment. 'Yes – I should,' he admitted. 'But I'm still ready to go. I'll do my very best if you'd like me to try. After all – it's me or nobody. You won't let Anne go – and there's not enough room for George and Timmy – and not enough for either you or Julian, Dick.'

Everyone was astonished. It didn't seem a bit like Richard to offer to do an unselfish or courageous action. Julian felt very doubtful.

'Well – this is a serious thing, you know, Richard,' he said. 'I mean – if you're going to do it, you've got to do it properly – go right through with it – not get frightened in the middle and begin howling, so that the men hear you and examine the boot.'

'I know,' said Richard. 'I think I can do it all right. I do wish you'd trust me a bit.'

'I can't understand your offering to do a difficult thing like that,' said Julian. 'It doesn't seem a bit like you – you've not shown yourself to be at all plucky *so* far!'

'Julian, I think *I* understand,' said Anne suddenly, and

she pulled at her brother's sleeve. 'He's thinking of *our* skins this time, not of his own – or at least he's trying to. Let's give him a chance to show he's got a bit of courage.'

'I only just want a chance,' said Richard in a small voice.

'All right,' said Julian. 'You shall have it. It'll be a very pleasant surprise if you take your chance and do something helpful!'

'Tell me exactly what I've got to do,' said Richard, trying to keep his voice from trembling.

'Well – once you're in the boot we'll have to shut you in. Goodness knows how long you'll have to wait there in the dark,' said Julian. 'I warn you it will be jolly stuffy and uncomfortable. When the car goes off it will be more uncomfortable still.'

'Poor Richard,' said Anne.

'As soon as the car stops anywhere and you hear the men get out, wait a minute to give them time to get out of sight and hearing – and then scramble out of the boot yourself and go straight to the nearest police-station,' said Julian. 'Tell your story *quickly,* give this address – Owl's Dene, Owl's Hill, some miles from Middlecombe Woods – and the police will do the rest. Got all that?'

'Yes,' said Richard.

'Do you still want to go, now you know what you're in for?' asked Dick.

'Yes,' said Richard again. He was surprised by a warm hug from Anne.

'Richard, you're nice – and I didn't think you were!' said Anne.

He then got a thump on the back from Julian, 'Well, Richard – pull this off and you'll wipe out all the silly things you've done! Now – what about getting into the boot immediately? We don't know when the men will be coming out.'

'Yes. I'll get in now,' said Richard, feeling remarkably

brave after Anne's hug and Julian's thump. Julian opened the boot. He examined the inside of the boot-cover. 'I don't believe Richard could open it from the inside,' he said. 'No, he couldn't. We mustn't close it tight, then – I'll have to wedge it a bit open with a stick or something. That will give him a little air, and he'll be able to push the boot open when he wants to. Where's a stick?'

Dick found one. Richard got into the boot and curled himself up. There wasn't very much room even for him!

He looked extremely cramped. Julian shut the boot and wedged it with a stick so that there was a crack of half an inch all round.

Dick gave him a sharp nudge. 'Quick – someone's coming!'

18

Hunt for Richard!

Mr Perton could be seen standing at the front door, outlined in the light from the lamp in the hall. He was talking to Rooky, who, apparently, was not going out. It seemed as if only Mr Perton was leaving in the car.

'Good luck, Richard,' Julian whispered, as he and the others melted into the shadows on the other side of the drive. They stood there in the darkness, watching Mr Perton walk over to the car. He got in and slammed the door. Thank goodness he hadn't wanted to put anything in the boot!

The engine started up and the car purred away down the drive. At the same time there came the grating sound of the gate machinery being used.

'Gates are opening for him,' muttered Dick. They heard the car go right down the drive and out of the gateway without stopping. It hooted as it went, evidently a signal to the house. The gates had been opened just at the right moment. They were now being shut, judging by the grinding noise going on.

The front door closed. The children stood in silence for a minute or two, thinking of Richard shut up in the boot.

'I'd never have thought it of him,' said George.

'No – but you just simply never know what is in anybody,' said Julian thoughtfully. 'I suppose even the worst coward, the most despicable crook, the most dishonest rogue *can* find some good thing in himself if he wants to badly enough.'

'Yes – it's the "wanting-to" that must be so rare, though,' said Dick. 'Look – there's Aggie at the kitchen-door. She's calling us in.'

They went to her. 'You can come in now,' she said. 'I can't give you much supper, I'm afraid, because Hunchy will be here – but I'll put some cake up in your room, under the blankets.'

They went into the kitchen. It was pleasant with a log-fire and the mellow light from an oil-lamp. Hunchy was at the far end doing something with a rag and polish. He gave the children one of his familiar scowls. 'Take that dog out and leave him out,' he ordered.

'No,' said George.

'Then I'll tell Rooky,' said Hunchy. Neither he nor Aggie seemed to notice that there were only four children, not five.

'Well, if Rooky comes here I've no doubt Timmy will bite his other hand,' said George. 'Anyway – won't he be surprised to find Timmy still alive and kicking?'

Nothing more was said about Timmy. Aggie silently put the remains of a plum-pie on the table. 'There's your supper,' she said.

There was a very small piece each. As they were finishing, Hunchy went out. Aggie spoke in a whisper.

'I heard the wireless at six o'clock. There was a police message about one of you – called Richard. His mother reported him missing – and the police put it out on the wireless.'

'Did they really?' said Dick. 'I say – they'll soon be here then!'

'But do they know where you are?' asked Aggie, surprised. Dick shook his head.

'Not yet – but I expect we'll soon be traced here.'

Aggie looked doubtful. 'Nobody's ever been traced here yet – nor ever will be, it's my belief. The police did come once, looking for somebody, and Mr Perton let them in, all polite-like. They hunted everywhere for the person they said they wanted, but they couldn't find him.'

Julian nudged Dick. He thought *he* knew where the police might have found him – in the little secret room behind that sliding panel.

'Funny thing,' said Julian. 'I haven't seen a telephone here. Don't they have one?'

'No,' said Aggie. 'No phone, no gas, no electricity, no water laid on, no nothing. Only just secrets and signs and comings and goings and threats and . . .'

She broke off as Hunchy came back, and went to the big fire-place, where a kettle was slung over the burning logs. Hunchy looked round at the children.

'Rooky wants the one of you that's called Richard,' he said, with a horrible smile. 'Says he wants to learn him a few lessons.'

All the four felt extremely thankful that Richard was not there. They felt sure he wouldn't have liked the lessons that Rooky wanted to teach him.

They looked round at one another and then all round the room. 'Richard? Where *is* Richard?'

'What do you mean – where's Richard?' said Hunchy, in a snarling voice that made Timmy growl. 'One of you is Richard – that's all I know.'

'Why – there were five children – now there's only four!' said Aggie, in sudden astonishment. 'I've only just noticed. Is Richard the missing one?'

'Dear me – *where's* Richard gone?' said Julian, pretending to be surprised. He called him 'Richard! Hey, Richard, where are you?'

Hunchy looked angry. 'Now, none of your tricks. One of you's Richard. Which one?'

'Not one of us is,' answered Dick. 'Gracious, where *can* Richard be? Do you suppose we've left him in the grounds, Ju?'

'Must have,' said Julian. He went to the kitchen window and swung it wide open. 'RICHARD!' he roared. 'You're wanted, RICHARD!'

But no Richard answered or appeared, of course. He was miles away in the boot of the black Bentley!

There came the sound of angry footsteps in the hall and the kitchen door was flung open. Rooky stood there, scowling, his hand done up in a big bandage. With a delighted bark Timmy leapt forward. George caught him just in time.

'That dog! Didn't I say he was to be poisoned?' shouted Rooky, furiously. 'Why haven't you brought that boy to me, Hunchy?'

Hunchy looked afraid. 'He don't seem to be here,' he answered sullenly. 'Unless one of these here children is him, sir.'

Rooky glanced over them. 'No – he's not one of them. Where is Richard?' he demanded of Julian.

'I've just been yelling for him,' said Julian, with an air of amazement. 'Funny thing. He was out in the grounds all day with us – and now we're indoors, he just isn't here. Shall I go and hunt in the grounds?'

'I'll shout for him again,' said Dick, going to the window. 'RICHARD!'

'Shut up!' said Rooky. '*I'll* go and find him. Where's my torch? Get it, Aggie. And when I find him – he'll be sorry for himself, very, very sorry!'

'I'll come too,' said Hunchy. 'You go one way and I'll go another.'

'Get Ben and Fred too,' ordered Rooky. Hunchy departed to fetch Ben and Fred, whoever they were. The children supposed they must be the other men who had arrived with Rooky the night before.

Rooky went out of the kitchen door with his powerful torch. Anne shivered. She was very, very glad that Richard couldn't be found, however hard the men looked for him. Soon there came the sound of other voices in the grounds, as the four men separated into two parties, and began to search every yard.

'Where is he, the poor boy?' whispered Aggie.

'I don't know,' said Julian, truthfully. He wasn't going to give any secrets away to Aggie, even though she seemed really friendly to them.

She went out of the room and the children clustered together, speaking in low voices.

'I *say* – what a blessing it was Richard that went off in the Bentley and not one of *us*,' whispered George.

'My word, yes – I didn't like the look on Rooky's face when he came into the kitchen just now,' said Julian.

'Well, Richard's got a little reward for trying to be brave,' said Anne. 'He's missed some ill-treatment from Rooky!'

Julian glanced at a clock in the kitchen. 'Look – it's almost nine. There's a wireless on that shelf. Let's put it on and see if there's a message about Richard.'

He switched it on and twiddled the knob till he got the right station. After a minute or two of news, there came the message they wanted to hear.

'Missing from home since Wednesday, Richard Thurlow Kent, a boy of twelve, well-built, fair hair, blue eyes, wearing grey shorts and grey jersey. Probably on a bicycle.'

So the message went on, ending with a police telephone number that could be called. There was of course no message about Julian and the others. They were relieved. 'That means that Mother won't be worrying,' said George. 'But it also means that unless Richard can get help nobody can possibly find out we're here – if we're not missed we can't be searched for, and I don't really want to be here much longer.'

Nobody did, of course. All their hopes were now on Richard. He seemed rather a broken reed to rely on – but you never knew! He just might be successful in escaping unseen from the boot and getting to a police station.

After about an hour Rooky and the others came in, all in a furious temper. Rooky turned on Julian.

'What's happened to that boy? You must know.'

'Gr-r-r-r-r,' said Timmy at once. Rooky beckoned to Julian to come into the hall. He shut the kitchen door and shouted at Julian again.

'Well – you heard what I said – where's that boy?'

'Isn't he out in the grounds?' said Julian, putting on a very perturbed look. 'Good gracious – what *can* have happened to him? I assure you he was with us all day. Aggie will tell you that – and Hunchy too.'

'They've already told me,' said Rooky. 'He's not in the grounds. We've gone over every inch. Where is he?'

'Well, would he be somewhere in the house, then?' suggested Julian, innocently.

'How can he be?' raged Rooky. 'The front door's been closed and locked all day except when Perton went out. And Hunchy and Aggie swear he didn't come into the kitchen.'

'It's an absolute mystery,' said Julian. 'Shall I hunt all over the house? The others can help me. Maybe the dog will smell him out.'

'I'm not having that dog out of the kitchen,' said Rooky. 'Or any of *you*, either! I believe that boy's about somewhere, laughing up his sleeve at us all – and I believe you know where he is too!'

'I don't,' said Julian. 'And that's the truth.'

'When I *do* find him, I'll . . . I'll . . .' Rooky broke off, quite unable to think of anything bad enough to do to poor Richard.

He went to join the others, still muttering. Julian went thankfully back to the kitchen. He was very glad Richard was well out of the way. It was pure chance that he had gone – but what a very good thing! Where was Richard now? What was he doing? Was he still in the boot of the car? How Julian wished he knew!

19

Richard has his own adventure

Richard had been having a much too exciting time. He had gone with the car, of course, crouching in the boot at the back, with a box of tools digging into him, and a can of petrol smelling horribly nearby, making him feel sick.

Through the gates went the car, and down the hill. It went at a good pace, and once stopped very suddenly. It had gone round a corner and almost collided with a stationary lorry, so that Mr Perton put the brake on in a hurry. Poor Richard was terrified. He bumped his head hard on the back of the boot and gave a groan.

He sat curled up, feeling sick and scared. He began to wish he had not tried to be a hero and get help. Being any kind of a hero was difficult – but this was a dreadful way of being heroic.

The car went on for some miles; Richard had no idea where it was going. At first he heard no other traffic at all – then he heard the sound of many wheels on the road, and knew he must be getting near a town. Once they must have gone by a railway station or railway line because Richard could distinctly hear the noise of a train, and then a loud hooting.

The car stopped at last. Richard listened intently. Was it stopping just for traffic lights – or was Mr Perton getting out? If so, that was his chance to escape!

He heard the car door slam. Ah – Mr Perton was out of the car then. Richard pressed hard at the cover of the boot. Julian had wedged it rather tightly, but it gave at last, and the lid of the boot opened. It fell back with rather a noise.

Richard looked out cautiously. He was in a dark street. A few people were walking on the pavement opposite. A lamp-post was some way away. Could he get out now – or would Mr Perton be about and see him?

He stretched out a leg to slide from the boot and jump to the ground – but he had been huddled up in an awkward position for so long that he was too stiff to move. Cramp caught him and he felt miserably uncomfortable as he tried to straighten himself out.

Instead of jumping out and taking to his heels at once, poor Richard had to go very slowly indeed. His legs and arms would *not* move quickly. He sat for a half-minute on the open boot-lid, trying to make up his mind to jump down.

And then he heard Mr Perton's voice! He was running down the steps of the house outside which he had parked the car. Richard was horrified. It hadn't dawned on him that he would come back so quickly.

He tried to jump from the boot-cover, and fell sprawling to the ground. Mr Perton heard him, and, thinking some-one was trying to steal something from his car he rushed up to the boot.

Richard scrambled up just in time to get away from his outstretched hand. He ran to the other side of the road as fast as he could, hoping that his stiff, cramped legs wouldn't let him down. Mr Perton tore after him.

'Hey, you, stop! What are you doing in my car?' shouted Mr Perton. Richard dodged a passer-by and tore on, panic-stricken. He mustn't be caught; he mustn't be caught!

Mr Perton caught up with him just under the lamp-post. He grabbed Richard's collar and swung him round roughly. 'You let me go!' yelled Richard, and kicked Mr Perton's ankles so hard that he almost fell over.

Mr Perton recognized him! 'Good gracious – it's you!' he cried. 'The boy Rooky wants! What are you doing here? How did you . . .?'

But with a last despairing struggle, Richard was off again, leaving his coat in Mr Perton's hands! His legs were feeling better now, and he could run faster.

He tore round the corner, colliding with another boy. He was off and away before the boy could even call out. Mr Perton also tore round the corner and collided with the same boy – who, however, was a bit quicker than before, and clutched Mr Perton by the coat, in a real rage at being so nearly knocked over again.

By the time Mr Perton had got himself free from the angry boy, Richard was out of sight. Mr Perton raced to the corner of the road, and looked up and down the poorly lighted road. He gave an exclamation of anger.

'Lost him! Little pest – how did he get here? Could he have been at the back of the car? Ah – surely that's him over there!'

It was. Richard had hidden in a garden, but was now being driven out by the barking of a dog. In despair he tore out of the gate and began running again. Mr Perton tore after him.

Round another corner, panting hard. Round yet another, hoping that no passer-by would clutch at him and stop him. Poor Richard! He didn't feel at all heroic, and didn't enjoy it a bit either.

He stumbled round the next corner and came into the main street of the town – and there, opposite, was a lamp that had a very welcome word shining on the glass.

POLICE

Thankfully Richard stumbled up the steps and pushed open the police station door. He almost fell inside. There was a kind of waiting-room there with a policeman sitting at a table. He looked up in astonishment as Richard came in in such a hurry.

'Now then – what's all this?' he asked the boy.

Richard looked fearfully back at the door, expecting Mr Perton to come in at any moment. But he didn't. The door remained shut. Mr Perton was not going to visit any police station if he could help it – especially with Richard pouring out a most peculiar story!

Richard was panting so much that he couldn't say a word at first. Then it all came out. The policeman listened in amazement, and very soon stopped Richard's tale, and called a big burly man in, who proved to be a most important police inspector.

He made Richard tell his tale slowly and as clearly as he could. The boy was now feeling much better – in fact he was feeling quite proud of himself! To think he'd done it – escaped in the boot of the car – got out – managed to get away from Mr Perton – and arrive safely at the police station. Marvellous!

'Where's this Owl's Dene?' demanded the Inspector, and the constable near by answered.

'Must be that old place on Owl's Hill, sir. You remember we once went there on some kind of police business, but it seemed to be all right. Run by a hunch-back and his sister for some man who is often away abroad – Perton, I think the name was.'

'That's right!' cried Richard. 'It was Mr Perton's car I came here in – a black Bentley.'

'Know the number?' said the Inspector, sharply.

KMF 102,' said Richard at once.

'Good lad,' said the Inspector. He picked up a telephone and gave a few curt instructions for a police car to try to trace the Bentley immediately.

'So you're Richard Thurlow Kent,' he said. 'Your mother is very upset and anxious about you. I'll see that she is telephoned to straight away. You'd better be taken home now in a police car.'

'Oh but, sir – can't I go with you to Owl's Dene when

you drive up there?' said Richard, deeply disappointed. 'You'll be going there, won't you? – because of all the others – Anne, Dick, George and Julian.'

'We'll be going all right,' said the Inspector, grimly. 'But you won't be with us. You've had enough adventures. You can go home and go to bed. You've done well to escape and come here. Quite the hero!'

Richard couldn't help feeling pleased – but how he wished he could race off to Owl's Dene with the police. What a marvellous thing it would be to march in with them and show Julian how well he had managed his part of the affair! Perhaps Julian would think better of him then.

The Inspector, however, was not having any boys in the cars that were to go to Owl's Dene, and Richard was taken off by the young constable, and told to wait till a car came to take him home.

The telephone rang, and the Inspector answered it. 'No trace of the Bentley? Right. Thanks.'

He spoke to the young constable. 'Didn't think they'd get him. He's probably raced back to Owl's Dene to warn the others.'

'We'll get there soon after!' said the constable with a grin. 'Our Wolseley's pretty well as fast as a Bentley!'

Mr Perton had indeed raced off, as soon as he saw Richard stumbling up the police station steps. He had gone back to his car at top speed, jumped in, slammed the door and raced away as fast as he could, feeling certain that the police would be on the look-out for KMF 102 immediately.

He tore dangerously round the corners, and hooted madly, making everyone leap out of the way. He was soon out in the country, and there he put on terrific speed, his powerful headlights picking out the dark country lanes for half a mile ahead.

As he came to the hill on which Owl's Dene stood, he

hooted loudly. He wanted the gates opened quickly! Just as he got up to them they opened. Someone had heard his hooting signal – good! He raced up the drive and stopped at the front door. It opened as he jumped out. Rooky stood there, and two other men with him, all looking anxious.

'What's up, Perton? Why are you back so quickly?' called Rooky. 'Anything wrong?''

Mr Perton ran up the steps, shut the door and faced the three men in the hall.

'Do you know what's happened? That boy, Richard Kent, was in the car when I went out! See? Hidden in the back or in the boot, or somewhere! Didn't you miss him?'

'Yes,' said Rooky. 'Of course we missed him. Did you let him get away, Perton?'

'Well, seeing that I didn't know he was in hiding, and had to leave the car to go in and see Ted, it was easy for him to get away!' said Mr Perton. 'He ran like a hare. I nearly grabbed him once, but he wriggled out of his coat. And as he ended up finally in the police station I decided to give up the chase and come back to warn you.'

'The police will be out here then, before you can say Jack Robinson,' shouted Rooky. 'You're a fool, Perton – you ought to have got that boy. There's our ransom gone west – and I was so glad to be able to get my hands on the little brute.'

'It's no good crying over spilt milk,' said Perton. 'What about Weston? Suppose the police find *him*. They're looking for him all right – the papers have been full of only two things the last couple of days – Disappearance of Richard Thurlow Kent – and Escape from Prison of Solomon Weston! And we're mixed up with both these. Do you want to be shoved back into prison again, Rooky? You've only just come out, you know. What are we going to do?'

'We must think,' said Rooky, in a panic-stricken voice. 'Come in this room here. We must *think*.'

20

The secret room

The four children had heard the car come racing up the drive, and had heard Mr Perton's arrival. Julian went to the kitchen door, eager to find out what he could. If Mr Perton was back, then either Richard had played his part well, and had escaped – or he had been discovered, and had been brought back.

He heard every word of the excited talk out in the hall. Good, good good! – Richard had got away – and was even now telling his tale to the police. It surely wouldn't be very long before the police arrived at Owl's Dene then – and what surprising things they would find there!

He tiptoed out into the hall, when he heard the men go into the room near by. What were their plans? He hoped they would not vent their rage on him or the others. It was true they had Timmy – but in a real emergency Rooky would probably think nothing of shooting the dog straightaway.

Julian didn't at all like what he heard from the room where the men talked over their plans.

'I'm going to bang all those kids' heads together as hard as I can, to start with,' growled Rooky. 'That big boy – what's his name? – Julian or something – must have planned Richard Kent's escape – I'll give him a real good thrashing, the interfering little beast.'

'What about the sparklers, Rooky?' said another man's voice. 'We'd better put them in a safe hidingplace before the police arrive. We'll have to hurry.'

'Oh, it'll be some time before they find they can't open that gate,' said Rooky. 'And it'll take a little more time before they climb that wall. We'll have time to put the sparklers into the room with Weston. If *he's* safe there, they'll be safe too.'

'Sparklers!' thought Julian, excited. 'Those are diamonds – so they've got a haul of diamonds hidden somewhere. Whatever next?'

'Get them,' ordered Mr Perton. 'Take them to the Secret Room – and be quick about it, Rooky. The police may be here at any minute now.'

'We'll spin some tale about that kid Richard and his friends,' said the voice of a fourth man. 'We'll say they were caught trespassing, the lot of them, and kept here as a little punishment. Actually, if there's time, I think it would be best to let the rest of them go. After all – they don't *know* anything. They can't give away any secrets.'

Rooky didn't want to let them go. He had grim plans for them, but the others argued him over. 'All right,' he said sullenly. 'Let them go, then – if there's time! You take them down to the gate, Perton, and shove them out before the police arrive. They'll probably set off thankfully and get lost in the dark. So much the better.'

'You get the sparklers then, and see to them,' said Mr Perton, and Julian heard him getting up from his chair. The boy darted back to the kitchen.

It looked as if there would be nothing for it but to let themselves be led down to the gates and shoved out and

Julian decided that if that happened they would wait at the gateway till the police arrived. They wouldn't get lost in the dark, as Rooky hoped!

Mr Perton came into the kitchen. His eyes swept over the four children. Timmy growled.

'So you made a little plan, did you, and hid Richard in the car?' he said. 'Well, for that we're going to turn you all out into the night – and you'll probably lose yourselves for days in the deserted countryside round here – and I hope you do!'

Nobody said anything. Mr Perton aimed a blow at Julian, who ducked. Timmy sprang at the man, but George had hold of his collar, and he just missed snapping Mr Perton's arm in two!

'If that dog had stayed here a day longer I'd have shot him,' said Mr Perton, fiercely. 'Come on, all of you, get a move on.'

'Good-bye, Aggie,' said Anne. Aggie and Hunchy watched them go out of the kitchen door into the dark garden. Aggie looked very scared indeed. Hunchy spat after them and said something rude.

But, when they were half-way down the drive, there came the sound of cars roaring at top speed up the hill to the gates of Owl's Dene! Two cars, fast and powerful, with brilliant headlights. Police cars, without a doubt! Mr Perton stopped. Then he shoved the children roughly back towards the house. It was too late to set them free and hope they would lose themselves.

'You look out for Rooky,' he said to them. 'He goes mad when he's frightened – and he's going to be frightened now, with the police hammering at the gates!'

Julian and the others cautiously edged into the kitchen. They weren't going to risk meeting Rooky if they could help it. Nobody was there at all, not even Hunchy or Aggie. Mr Perton went through to the hall.

'Have you put those sparklers away?' he called, and a

voice answered him: 'Yes. Weston's got them with him. They're O.K. Did you get the kids out in time?'

'No – and the police are at the gates already,' growled Mr Perton.

A howl came from someone – probably Rooky. 'The police – already! If I had that kid Richard here I'd skin him alive. Wait till I've burnt a few letters I don't want found – then I'll go and get hold of the other kids. I'm going to put somebody through it for this, and I don't care who.'

'Don't be foolish, Rooky,' said Mr Perton's voice. 'Do you want to get yourself into trouble again through your violent temper? Leave the kids alone.'

Julian listened to all this and felt very uneasy indeed. He ought to hide the others. Even Timmy would be no protection if Rooky had a gun. But where could he hide them?

'Rooky will search the whole house from top to bottom if he loses his temper much more, and really makes up his mind to revenge himself on us,' thought Julian. 'What a pity there isn't another secret room – we could hide there and be safe!'

But even if there was one he didn't know of it. He heard Rooky go upstairs with the others. Now, if he and the other children were going to hide somewhere in safety, this was their chance. But WHERE could they hide?

An idea came to Julian – was it a brilliant one, or wasn't it? He couldn't make up his mind at first. Then he decided that brilliant or not they had got to try it.

He spoke to the others. 'We've got to hide. Rooky isn't safe when he's in a temper.'

'Where shall we hide?' said Anne, fearfully.

'In the secret room!' said Julian. They all gaped at him in amazement.

'But – but somebody else is already hidden there – you told us you saw him last night,' said George at last.

'I know. That can't be helped. He's the last person to give us away, if we share his hiding-place – he wouldn't want to be found himself!' said Julian. 'It will be a frightful squash, because the secret room is very, very small – but it's the safest place I can think of.'

'Timmy will have to come too,' said George firmly. Julian nodded.

'Of course. We may need him to protect us against the hidden man!' he said. 'He may be pretty wild at us all invading his hiding-place. We don't want to have him calling Rooky. We'll be all right once we're in the room, because Timmy will keep him quiet. And once we're in he won't call out because we'll tell him the police are here!'

'Fine,' said Dick. 'Let's go. Is the coast clear?'

'Yes. They're all upstairs for some reason or other,' said Julian. 'Probably destroying things they don't want found. Come on.'

Hunchy and Aggie were still not to be seen. They had probably heard what the scare was about and were hidden away themselves! Julian led the way quietly to the little study.

They stared at the big, solid wooden bookcase that stretched from floor to ceiling. Julian went quickly to one shelf and emptied out the books. He felt for the knob.

There it was! He pulled it out, and the back panel of the shelf slid noiselessly downwards, leaving the large hole there, like a window into the secret room.

The children gasped. How queer! How very extraordinary! They blinked through the hole and saw the small room behind, lit by a little candle. They saw the hidden man too – and he saw them! He looked at them in the very greatest astonishment.

'Who are you?' he said, in a threatening voice. 'Who told you to open that panel? Where's Rooky and Perton?'

'We're coming through to join you,' said Julian quietly. 'Don't make a noise.'

He shoved George up first. She slid through the narrow opening sideways and landed feet-first on the floor. Timmy followed immediately, pushed through by Julian.

The man was up on his feet now, angry and surprised. He was a big burly fellow, with very small close-set eyes and a cruel mouth.

'Now look here,' he began in a loud voice. 'I won't have this. Where's Perton? Hey, Per . . .'

'If you say another word I'll set my dog on you,' said George, at a sign from Julian. Timmy growled so ferociously that the man shrank back at once.

'I – I . . .' he began. Timmy growled again and bared all his magnificent teeth in a snarl. The man climbed up on the narrow bed and subsided, looking astonished and furious. Dick went through the opening next, then Anne. By that time the small room was uncomfortably crowded.

'I say,' said Julian, suddenly remembering something, 'I shall have to stay outside the room – because the books have got to be put back, otherwise Rooky will notice the shelf is empty and guess we're hiding in the secret room. Then we'll be at his mercy.'

'Oh Ju – you must come in with us,' said Anne, frightened.

'I can't, Anne. I must shut the panel and put the books back,' said Julian. 'I can't risk your being discovered till the police have safely caught that madman Rooky! I shall be all right, don't you worry.'

'The police?' whispered the man in the secret room, his eyes almost falling out of his head. 'Are the police here?'

'At the gates,' answered Julian. 'So keep quiet if you don't want them on top of you at once!'

He pushed the knob. The panel slid back into place without a sound. Julian replaced the books on the shelf as fast as he could. Then he darted out of the study, so that the men would not even guess what he had been up to. He was very thankful that Rooky had kept away long enough for him to carry out his plan.

Where should he hide himself? How long would it take the police to get over the wall, or break down the great gates? Surely they would soon be here?

There came the sound of footsteps running down the stairs. It was Rooky. He caught sight of Julian at once. 'Ah – there you are! Where are the others? I'll show you what happens to children who upset my plans. I'll show you what . . .'

Rooky carried a whip in his hand and looked quite crazy. Julian was afraid. He darted back into the study and locked the door. Rooky began to hammer at it. Then such a crash came on the door that Julian guessed he was smashing it down with one of the hall chairs. The door would be down in a moment!

21

A very exciting finish!

Julian was a courageous boy, but just at that minute he felt very scared indeed. And what must the children hidden in the secret room beyond be thinking? Poor Anne must be feeling terrified at Rooky's shouts and the crashing on the door.

And then a really marvellous idea came to Julian. Why, oh why hadn't he thought of it before? He could open the gates himself for the police to come in! He knew how to do it – and there was the wheel nearby in the corner, that set the gate machinery working! Once he had the gates open it would not be more than a few minutes, surely, before the police were hammering at the front door.

Julian ran to the wheel-like handle. He turned it strongly. A grinding, whining noise came at once, as the machinery went into action.

Rooky was still crashing at the door with the heavy chair. Already he had broken in one panel of it. But when he suddenly heard the groaning of the machinery that opened the gates, he stopped in panic. The gates were being opened! The police would soon be there – he would be caught!

He forgot the beautiful stories he had arranged to tell, forgot the plans that he and the others had made, forgot everything except that he must hide. He flung down the chair and fled.

Julian sat down in the nearest chair, his heart beating as if he had just been running a race. The gates were open – Rooky had fled – the police would soon be there! And, even as he sat thinking this, there came the sound of powerful cars roaring up the wide drive. Then the engines stopped, and car doors were thrown open.

Someone began to hammer at the front door. 'Open in the name of the law!' cried a loud voice, and then came another hammering.

Nobody opened the door. Julian unlocked the half-broken door of the study he was in, and peered cautiously into the hall. No one seemed to be about.

He raced to the front door, pulled back the bolts, and undid the heavy chain, afraid each moment that some of the men would come to punch him away. But they didn't.

The door was pushed open by the police, who swarmed in immediately. There were eight of them, and they looked surprised to see a boy there.

'Which boy's this?' said the Inspector.

'Julian, sir,' said Julian. 'I'm glad you've come. Things were getting pretty hot.'

'Where are the men?' asked the Inspector, walking right in.

'I don't know,' said Julian.

'Find them,' ordered the Inspector, and his men fanned out up the hall. But before they could go into any room, a cool voice called to them from the end of the corridor.

'May I ask what all this is?'

It was Mr Perton, looking as calm as could be, smoking a cigarette. He stood at the door of his sitting-room,

seeming quite unperturbed. 'Since when has a man's house been broken into for no reason at all?'

'Where are the rest of you?' demanded the Inspector.

'In here, Inspector,' drawled Mr Perton. 'We were having a little conference, and heard the hammering at the door. Apparently you got in somehow. I'm afraid you'll get into trouble for this.'

The Inspector advanced to the room where Mr Perton stood. He glanced into it.

'Aha – our friend Rooky, I see,' he said, genially. 'Only a day or two out of prison, Rooky, and you're mixed up in trouble again. Where's Weston?'

'I don't know what you mean,' said Rooky, sullenly. 'How should I know where he is? He was in prison last time I knew anything about him.'

'Yes. But he escaped,' said the Inspector. 'Somebody helped him, Rooky. Somebody planned his escape for him – friends of yours – and somebody knows where the diamonds are that he stole and hid. I've a guess that you're going to share them with him in return for getting your friends to help him. Where is Weston, Rooky?'

'I tell you I don't *know*,' repeated Rooky. 'Not here, if that's what you're getting at. You can search the whole house from top to bottom, if you like. Perton won't mind. Will you, Perton? Look for the sparklers, too, if you want to. I don't know anything about them.'

'Perton, we've suspected you for a long time,' said the Inspector, turning to Mr Perton, who was still calmly smoking his cigarette. 'We think you're at the bottom of all these prison escapes – that's why you bought this lonely old house, isn't it? – so that you could work from it undisturbed? You arrange the escapes, you arrange for a change of clothes, you arrange for a safe hiding-place till the man can get out of the country.'

'Utter nonsense,' said Mr Perton.

'And you only help criminals who have been known to do a clever robbery and hide the stuff before they're caught,' went on the Inspector, in a grim voice. 'So you know you'll make plenty of profit on your deals Perton. Weston is here all right – and so are the diamonds. Where are they?'

'They're not here,' said Perton. 'You're at liberty to

149

look and see. You won't get anything out of *me*, Inspector. I'm innocent.'

Julian had listened to all this in amazement. Why, they had fallen into the very middle of a nest of thieves and rogues! Well – *he* knew where Weston was – and the diamonds too! He stepped forward.

'Tell your story later, son,' said the Inspector. 'We've things to do now.'

'Well, sir – I can save you a lot of time,' said Julian. 'I know where the hidden prisoner is – and the diamonds too!'

Rooky leapt to his feet with a howl. Mr Perton looked at Julian hard. The other men glanced uneasily at one another.

'You don't know anything!' shouted Rooky. 'You only came here yesterday.'

The Inspector regarded Julian gravely. He liked this boy with the quiet manners and honest eyes.

'Do you mean what you say?' he asked.

'Oh yes,' said Julian. 'Come with me, sir.'

He turned and went out of the room. Everyone crowded after him – police, Rooky and the others; but three of the policemen quietly placed themselves at the back.

Julian led them to the study. Rooky's face went purple, but Perton gave him a sharp nudge and he said nothing. Julian went to the bookcase and swept a whole shelf of books out at once.

Rooky gave a terrific yell and leapt at Julian. 'Stop that! What are you doing?'

Two policemen were on the infuriated Rooky at once. They dragged him back. Julian pulled out the knob and the panel slid noiselessly downwards, leaving a wide space in the wall behind.

From the secret room four faces gazed out – the faces of three children – and a man. Timmy was there too, but he was on the floor. For a few moments nobody said a single word. The ones in the hidden room were so surprised to see such a crowd of policemen looking in at them – and the ones in the study were filled with amazement to see so many children in the tiny room!

'WELL!' said the Inspector. 'Well, I'm blessed! And if that isn't Weston himself, large as life and twice as natural!'

Rooky began to struggle with the policemen. He seemed absolutely infuriated with Julian.

'That boy!' he muttered. 'Let me get at him. That boy!'

'Got the diamonds there, Weston?' asked the Inspector, cheerfully. 'May as well hand them over.'

Weston was very pale indeed. He made no move at all. Dick reached under the narrow bed and pulled out a bag. 'Here they are,' he said, with a grin. 'Jolly good lot they feel – heavy as anything! Can we come out now, Ju?'

All three were helped out by policemen. Weston was handcuffed before he was brought out. Rooky found that he also had handcuffs on all of a sudden, and to Mr Perton's angry surprise he heard a click at his own wrists too!

'A very, very nice little haul,' said the Inspector, in his most genial voice, as he looked inside the bag. 'What happened to your prison clothes, Weston? That's a nice suit you've got on – but you weren't wearing that when you left prison.'

'I can tell you where they are,' said Julian, remembering. Everyone stared in amazement, except George and Anne, who also knew, of course.

'They're stuffed down a well belonging to an old tumble-down shack on a lane between here and Middlecombe Woods,' said Julian. 'I could easily find it for you any time.'

Mr Perton stared at Julian as if he couldn't believe his ears. 'How do you know that?' he asked roughly. 'You can't know a thing like that!'

'I do know it,' said Julian. 'And what's more you took him a new suit of clothes, and arrived at the shack in your black Bentley, didn't you – KMF 102? I saw it.'

'That's got you, Perton,' said the Inspector, with a pleased smile. 'That's put you on the spot, hasn't it? Good boy, this – notices a whole lot of interesting things. I shouldn't be surprised if he joins the police force some day. We could do with people like him!'

Perton spat out his cigarette and stamped on it viciously, as if he wished he was stamping on Julian. Those children! If that idiot Rooky hadn't spotted Richard Kent and gone after him, none of this would have happened. Weston would have been safely hidden, the diamonds sold, Weston could have been sent abroad, and he, Perton, would have made a fortune. Now a pack of children had spoilt everything.

'Any other people in the house?' the Inspector asked Julian. 'You appear to be the one who knows more than anybody else, my boy – so perhaps you can tell me that.'

'Yes – Aggie and Hunchy,' said Julian, promptly. 'But don't be hard on Aggie, sir – she was awfully good to us, and she's terrified of Hunchy.'

'We'll remember what you say,' promised the Inspector. 'Search the house, men. Bring along Aggie and Hunchy too. We'll want them for witnesses, anyway. Leave two men on guard here. The rest of us will go.'

It needed the black Bentley as well as the two police cars to take everyone down the drive and on to the next town! The children's bicycles had to be left behind, as they could not be got on the cars anywhere. As it was, it was a terrific squash.

'You going home tonight?' the Inspector asked Julian. 'We'll run you back. What about your people? Won't they be worried by all this?'

'They're away,' explained Julian. 'And we were on a

cycling tour. So they don't know. There's really nowhere we can go for the night.'

But there was! There was a message awaiting the Inspector to say that Mrs Thurlow Kent would be very pleased indeed if Julian and the others would spend the night with Richard. She wanted to hear about their extraordinary adventures.

'Right,' said Julian. 'That settles that. We'll go there – and anyway, I want to bang old Richard on the back. He turned out quite a hero after all!'

'You'll have to keep around for a few days,' said the Inspector. 'We'll want you, I expect – you've a very fine tale to tell, and you've been a great help.'

'We'll keep around then,' said Julian. 'And if you could manage to have our bikes collected, sir, I'd be very grateful.'

Richard was at the front door to meet them all, although by now it was very late indeed. He was dressed in clean clothes and looked very spruce beside the dirty, bedraggled company of children that he went to greet.

'I wish I'd been in at the last!' he cried. 'I was sent off home, and I was wild. Mother – and Dad – here are the children I went off with.'

Mr Thurlow Kent had just come back from America. He shook hands with all of them. 'Come along in,' he said. 'We've got a fine spread for you – you must be ravenous!'

'Tell me what happened, tell me at once,' demanded Richard.

'We simply *must* have a bath first,' protested Julian. 'We're filthy.'

'Well, you can tell me while you're having a bath,' said Richard. 'I can't wait to hear!'

It was lovely to have hot baths and to be given clean clothes. George was solemnly handed out shorts like the boys, and the others grinned to see that both Mr and Mrs

Kent thought she was a boy. George, of course, grinned too, and didn't say a word.

'I was very angry with Richard when I heard what he had done,' said Mr Kent, when they were all sitting at table, eating hungrily. 'I'm ashamed of him.'

Richard looked downcast at once. He gazed beseechingly at Julian.

'Yes – Richard made a fool of himself,' said Julian. 'And landed us all into trouble. He wants taking in hand, sir.'

Richard looked even more downcast. He went very red, and looked at the table-cloth.

'But,' said Julian, 'he more than made up for his silliness, sir – he offered to squash himself into the boot of the car, and escape that way, and go and warn the police. That took some doing, believe me! I think quite a bit of Richard now!'

He leaned over and gave the boy a pat on the back. Dick and the others followed it up with thumps, and Timmy woofed in his deepest voice.

Richard was now red with pleasure. 'Thanks,' he said, awkwardly. 'I'll remember this.'

'See you do, my boy!' said his father. 'It might all have ended very differently!'

'But it didn't,' said Anne happily. 'It ended like this. We can all breathe again!'

'Till the next time,' said Dick, with a grin. 'What do *you* say, Timmy, old boy?'

'Woof,' said Timmy, of course, and thumped his tail on the floor. 'WOOF!'